Confessions, Hot Tubs & Second Chances

The Tropes Book #3

Tasha Zima

Ashby Lake Publishing House

Book Cover by Tasha Zima

ISBN: 978-1-0699810-3-5 (ebook)

ISBN: 978-1-06989810-4-2 (paperback)

Contents

To my husband, always.

Especially to my readers.
Without you, there would be no stories to tell.
Thank you.
A special thank you to Gigi and TC – your support and enthusiasm for my writing has kept me going.
You are both incredible women.

No One Is Surprised

Jonah knew his life was drifting in a direction he hadn't exactly chosen — more like a slow tugboat being pulled by everyone else's currents.

His twin brother? Running a wildly successful boat restoration business, practically engaged, already acting like a husband.

His older half brothers? Settled in their careers, in relationships that looked like they'd been carved out of Pinterest boards.

Even his *sort-of* sisters had their lives in gear — one was off on an Eat, Pray, Love pilgrimage and texting photos of herself meditating on cliff edges, and the other was blissfully wrapped up in her girlfriend, building a future with the quiet confidence he envied.

Meanwhile, Jonah... was still Jonah.

Smart, steady, helpful Jonah.

Floating Jonah.

He didn't feel unhappy. Just... stuck. Like life was a race and he'd politely stepped aside to let everyone else pass him.

He wanted something bold.

Something stupidly dramatic.

Something no one would see coming.

So he applied to be on Love North of 60, the new high-arctic romance experiment streaming on FrostByte+.

The one with:

- outdoor fire pits overlooking frozen lakes
- nightly sauna confessionals
- hot tubs half-buried in snow
- northern lights that danced like they were taunting you
- and a ridiculously eco-chic lodge made of cedar, glass, and the tears of minimalist architects

He'd filled out the application form on a whim at two in the morning, eating cold leftover lasagne straight from the container.

He didn't even upload a proper headshot — just a pic his sister Sabriana had taken during a family barbecue where he was squinting into the sun.

He was in a pair of surfer shorts, his blond hair had that perfect beach look and he had posed like a body builder, showing off his biceps. Which he had to admit, he looked good in that picture.

He never expected a call-back.

But then the casting producer emailed.

Then called.

Then squealed — actually squealed — when she learned he was a twin *("Do you both want to come on the show?")*.

Even when Jonah said no, he was the only one applying, she still sounded thrilled.

A week later, he had a contract.

He didn't tell his twin Caleb.

He simply announced to his family group chat that he'd be "traveling for a few weeks."

No one even responded with anything stronger than a thumbs-up emoji.

Apparently it wasn't weird or off-brand at all that Jonah was about disappear for a few weeks, by himself.

And for the first time in a long time... he felt *alive.*

The Show

Jonah wasn't a fan of reality dating shows.

Sure, he'd watched a couple episodes here and there — usually because a date wanted to *"just see the drama, it's so bad it's good."*

He'd always found the whole thing painfully contrived.

Forced chemistry.

Camera-ready heartbreak.

But when he finally arrived on set?

He realized he had *severely underestimated* just how contrived things could be.

Their entrances were staggered.

One contestant at a time, spaced out by fifteen minutes, so the cameras could get "first impressions" and "natural dynamics" (translation: manufactured drama) as cleanly as possible. Jonah was assigned the very last arrival slot.

Which meant the lodge was already buzzing by the time he stepped inside — a warm explosion of voices, laughter, clashing personalities, and the glow of overhead lights reflecting off floor-to-ceiling windows.

He stomped snow off his boots, adjusting the thick parka hood around his ears. The freezing air still pinned red to his cheeks.

A producer near the bar gestured sharply.

"There," she whispered, like she was feeding the wolves."

"Everyone, meet... Jonah!"

Every conversation stopped.

Eleven strangers turned toward him.

Faces curious.

Faces calculating.

Faces already forming opinions.

Jonah lifted a hand, gave a sheepish smile — and then—

CRASH.

A glass shattered somewhere near the fireplace.

Someone gasped.

Everyone's attention snapped away from him as sharply as it had landed.

Jonah blinked, confused — until he followed their line of sight.

And saw *her*.

Standing behind the kitchen island.

Frozen mid-step.

Holding nothing but shock.

Brittany Kildare.

His best friend from high school.

His everything for one night before her world broke.

The girl he hadn't seen in nine years.

Somehow she looked more beautiful and identical to what he remembered.

Her long, dark brown hair was pulled back in a ponytail, which made her cheekbones stand out even more. She sported a golden tan and a form fitting dress that showed Jonah exactly how much she had grown up.

Her lips parted.

Her dark brown eyes went wide.

And her voice — *oh God* — her voice was exactly the same.

"Jonah?"

His heart punched upward.

His breath vanished.

And despite the cameras, despite the crowd, despite every stupid choice that had led him to this moment...

His face split into the kind of grin he didn't plan, didn't control, didn't *ever* give to strangers.

"Britt?" he breathed, soft and thunderstruck.

The Reunion

Brittany hadn't seen Jonah in nine years.

Nine years since her mother took her last breath in a too-bright hospital room.

Nine years since Brittany had been packed off to Argentina to live with a father she barely knew — a man who swung between overprotective and emotionally absent, as if smothering her counted as parenting. Nine years since the night everything changed between them.

Those years were... a blur.

A lonely, frustrating, too-fast blur.

Internet access was spotty. Her father controlled the phone bills and refused to let her get a new sim card. Social media wasn't allowed — "dangerous," he'd said, though she'd always suspected he meant "distracting."

So she lost everyone.

Jonah.

Her other friends.

Her school.

Her sense of home.

By the time she had any autonomy again — a cheap phone, a way to get online, a place where she could breathe — years had passed.

People had moved on.

She didn't know how to step back into lives she'd fallen out of.

So she didn't.

She pushed forward instead.

A modelling scout found her at a street market in Buenos Aires.

Nothing glamorous but she made enough to carve her way out of Argentina and back to Canada.

And for a while, that felt like a victory.

But modelling came with its own kind of hollowness — the constant scrutiny, the fake smiles, the constant whisper of *be thinner, be prettier, be quieter.*

She wanted something real.

Something that mattered.

Something like the social work degree she'd once dreamed of back in high school, sitting beside Jonah during late-night homework sessions while he explained chemistry formulas in that patient way that had always undone her.

The prize money for Love North of 60 was enough to fund that dream.

And she knew how these shows worked.

She knew the archetypes.

She knew how to play the game while keeping enough walls up to protect herself.

What she didn't know — *not in her wildest imaginings* — was that stepping into this lodge, of all places, would mean stepping straight back into her past.

Straight back into the eyes she thought she'd never see again.

Straight back into Jonah.

On Camera

Brittany was just about to step forward—heart still rattling in her chest—when the producer suddenly threw her arms into the air.

"Cut! CUT! Oh my GOD. That was perfect."

She practically vibrated with glee. "You two are the focus of episode one. Who knew? Who *KNEW*?"

She clapped for someone to clean the broken glass, then ushered Brittany and Jonah to the side like they were VIPs being escorted to their thrones. The other contestants hovered, wide-eyed, blatantly eavesdropping, already sensing the main-character energy radiating off these two like northern lights on steroids.

"Okay, places! And—ROLL!"

Brittany swallowed. Her pulse thudded in her ears.

She was off her game.

Completely derailed.

She had walked into this lodge planning to be the villain from minute one—the icy, unbothered, camera-savvy girl who ate weaker contestants for breakfast and wore stilettos in the snow just to prove a point.

But this?

Seeing Jonah?

Having her entire heart kick-start like someone jump-scared her soul?

Not in the plan.

And the cameras were rolling.

She cleared her throat.

And then made a choice.

With a sharp snap of movement, she slapped Jonah across the face.

Not hard.

Just enough for the sound to crack through the lodge like a warning shot.

"You shouldn't be here," she hissed, planting her hands on her hips. "You broke my heart, you bastard."

A collective *ohhhhhhhhhh* rippled through the group.

Jonah... didn't flinch.

Of course he didn't.

He knew her.

He knew this wasn't real—but also... kind of was?

He also knew they were on television, and if Brittany Kildare was starting a scene, he wasn't going to leave her stranded in it.

So he slowly set his bag down at his feet.

Unzipped his parka.

Shrugged out of it in one smooth, deliberate motion.

The lodge air wasn't even that warm, but suddenly everyone else was sweating.

Because Jonah was wearing a black compression shirt.

The kind that clung.

Everywhere.

A few contestants actually *whistled.*

Someone muttered *"helloooo plot twist"* under their breath.

Jonah stepped toward her, closing the space until she had no choice but to tilt her chin up.

"I broke *your* heart?" he asked, voice low, teasing, dangerous in a way he'd never dared back in high school.

He leaned in—close enough that their noses almost brushed, close enough that she remembered the exact shape of his breath on cold mornings in the band hallway.

"Honey," he murmured, "I'm not the one who ran off to Argentina."

Then he straightened, cool as an iceberg sliding into the ocean... and *stalked off.*

Brittany's gasp cracked through the room like a firework.

The producer shrieked, "CUT!"

She clutched her clipboard to her chest as if it held the Holy Grail.

"This is going to be a DREAM SEASON," she whispered, starry-eyed. "A DREAM."

Nips

The rest of the evening played out exactly the way the producers wanted — and exactly the way Brittany had expected.

The dorm-style room selection?

Pure chaos disguised as "fun."

A PA handed out flimsy printed cards with their names on them, directing everyone to claim bunks like they were in a retro sleepaway camp crossed with a prison intake. The cameras zoomed in at every gasp, every exaggerated groan, every *"Oh my God, you snore? No way I'm above you."*

Then came the staged "arrival drinks," where the producer barked orders like a drill sergeant in skinny jeans.

"Stand closer!"

"No, closer than that!"

"Pretend you like each other!"

"Okay, now cheers — NO, NOT LIKE NORMAL PEOPLE. Bigger smiles! Bigger teeth!"

Someone knocked over a shot glass.

Someone else flirted with the wrong person.

There were at least four retakes.

The artificiality of it all clung to the air like cheap hairspray.

And then came the swimsuit directive.

The hot tub — a gigantic steaming crater carved into the snowy deck — sat just a metre or so from the back door.

But they weren't allowed robes, towels, or even hoodies.

"Skin sells," the producer had chirped unapologetically. "I want to see nips on everyone. Yes, I said nips. Move, move, move!"

Brittany had rolled her eyes so hard she nearly sprained something.

But she still changed into a sleek black bikini — high cut, minimal coverage, extremely camera-approved.

Jonah changed into dark swim trunks, the kind that should have been illegal on a man with shoulders like that.

By the time the group shuffled outside into the freezing air, everyone was yelping and cursing and hopping from foot to foot.

The second they slid into the steaming hot tub, a collective moan echoed around the deck. Warm water. Sanctuary. Blessed relief.

But for Brittany?

The heat had nothing to do with the temperature.

She and Jonah kept catching each other's eyes — then looking away, then looking back, as if pulled by magnets that had been dormant for years and were suddenly switched back on.

He'd grown up.

Broadened.

Sharpened.

Turned into a man who carried stillness like it was its own kind of power.

She'd grown up too — her edges refined, her confidence realer, her walls only half as impenetrable as she pretended.

And God, they liked what they saw.

The producer clapped her hands.

"All right! Time for intros!"

She pointed straight at them.

"Brittany and Jonah, you two will go last."

A ripple went through the tub.

Of course they would.

Of course.

And Brittany's heart—stupid, traitorous thing—thumped once, hard.

Hot Tub Introductions

Steam curled upward in soft white ribbons as everyone shifted around the massive hot tub, trying to find the least awkward position for being shoulder-to-shoulder with near-strangers in very small amounts of spandex.

The producer perched on a little stool with her clipboard like a wildlife photographer studying a herd of half-naked contestants in their natural mating habitat.

She raised her voice over the bubbling jets.

"Okay, everyone! Time for intros! Remember — fun, flirty, and around twenty seconds each. Viewers love authenticity, but not too much authenticity. Keep it aspirational. And smiling! Bigger! You're not freezing to death, you're HOT. And single!"

A few nervous giggles rippled around the circle.

"Let's start with... Tyler!"

Tyler — tall, blond, and resembling someone who exclusively ate protein powder — lifted his drink.

"Hey everyone, I'm Tyler, I'm 27, I'm a firefighter-slash-fitness-model from Edmonton—"

Of course he was.

"—and I'm here to find my northern soulmate!"

He winked. It was extremely rehearsed.

A few contestants clapped.

Jonah and Brittany did not.

They were sitting beside each other, bodies half-submerged, legs bumping under the water every so often as if fate was flicking them like dominoes and giggling.

Brittany pretended to sip her drink.

Jonah pretended to look at Tyler.

Both of them were liars.

The producer pointed at the next girl.

"Aaliyah!"

Aaliyah, gorgeous in a red bikini that set off her dark skin and curves to perfection, was already angling for the camera like she'd studied the geometry of seduction, leaned forward.

"I'm Aaliyah, 25, a beauty influencer from Montreal, and I am absolutely manifesting love under the northern lights!"

She tossed her hair.

A jet bubbled.

Someone wolf-whistled.

Jonah blinked once.

Brittany didn't even notice.

Because Jonah was too busy sliding a glance across the water.

And Brittany was too busy trying not to rediscover the exact shape of his mouth.

The intros kept coming.

"—mechanical engineer from Yellowknife—""—travel nurse who's sick of casual dating—""—snowboard instructor who loves poetry—"

But they may as well have been speaking underwater for all the attention those two paid.

Jonah's knee bumped Brittany's again under the surface.

She jolted.

He didn't apologize.

Their breaths synced.

Their eyes flicked up at the same moment.

The world shrank to a hot, steamy tunnel vision of *oh no, he's beautiful now* and *oh God, she grew up stunning.*

Their history sat between them like a live wire.

Electric.

Unaffordable.

Unavoidable.

The producer flipped a page on her clipboard.

"All right! And finally... Jonah and Brittany, you're up next!"

Every head turned toward them with barely disguised hunger for drama.

Brittany blinked like she'd just come up for air.

Jonah inhaled sharply, caught.

They had missed *every* intro.

And now?

Every camera in the room was pointed right at them.

Brittany pushed her wet hair off her shoulder, tilted her chin toward the camera, and delivered her line with the icy precision of someone who had practiced being unbothered in the mirror for years.

"I'm Brittany," she said, tone razor-sharp. "With a B like *Bitch.* Don't forget that. Most recently a model from Argentina."

The producer audibly choked on her own excitement.

Several contestants blinked.

One girl whispered "oh damn" behind her champagne flute.

Brittany gave the camera her most devastating villainess stare — eyebrows arched, jaw set, lips pouty but dangerous.

Jonah lasted exactly two seconds.

He burst out laughing.

Not polite laughing.

Not camera-appropriate laughing.

Real laughing — head thrown back, eyes crinkled, chest shaking, caught completely off guard.

It was joy.

Pure, uncontrollable joy.

The producer snapped her fingers at him so hard she could've summoned a demon.

"Shh!" she hissed.

"Composure, Jonah! COMPOSURE!"

He slapped a hand over his mouth, shoulders trembling, but his eyes were still warm and impossibly fond when he looked at Brittany.

He turned to the cameras, trying to recover.

"I'm Jonah," he said, voice deeper now, calmer, but undeniably amused. "I'm a twin. I'm bored with everything, so I thought I'd give this a try."

Then —He looked straight at Brittany.

Not a glance.

Not an accident.

A direct, purposeful, *lingering* stare.

Heat crawled up Brittany's neck.

Her cheeks flushed.

Her breath stuttered.

She tried to hide it, but the cameras were not her friends tonight.

"CUT!" the producer screamed.

"Oh my GOD, you two are GOLD."

She jabbed her pen toward them like it was a magic wand.

"Background footage! Move! Act like you're hotter than the hot tub!"

Contestants immediately shifted into chaotic posing mode — shoulders back, chests up, attempting smouldering looks while shivering violently under the water.

"We need a volunteer for the sauna confessional," the producer announced.

Trevor's hand shot up.

Of course it did.

"Great. Off you go.

"She waved him toward the cabin.

As he climbed out, everyone pretended not to stare at the water dripping down his abs.

But Brittany?

Jonah?

They only looked at each other.

Testing the Water

Everyone had moved around and Brittany made sure she was on the other side of the hot tub from Jonah.

"*Bitch,* huh?"

The guy from Yellowknife — broad shoulders, charming smile, and a very obvious desire to make screen time — slid into the space beside her as the woman next to him shifted over.

Brittany scrambled mentally for his name.

Wes? Will? Wade?

Something with a W.

She'd figure it out before the episode aired. Hopefully.

"Yes," she purred, letting her voice dip into her throat. "I like to push buttons."

To prove it, she lifted one wet fingertip and lazily traced it down his chest — a slow, teasing drag over warm skin and glistening droplets.

His eyes widened.

He leaned in just a little.

"I like that," he said, openly intrigued, maybe even impressed.

Brittany gave him a soft, fake pout.

"Oh," she huffed, lashes fluttering. "Then that's no fun."

She flipped her hair back with one fluid motion — all glimmering confidence and villain-queen theatrics — deliberately arching her back just enough to make the producer grin from her clipboard perch.

The contestants murmured.

Wes/Will/Wade swallowed.

And Jonah...Jonah had seen *enough.*

Without warning, a strong hand wrapped around Brittany's ankle under the water.

Her eyes widened.

She barely had time to gasp—

SPLASH.

Jonah yanked her toward him — and straight under the water — with a low, wicked smirk that sent a shockwave through the tub.

Chaos erupted.

A girl shrieked.

Someone's drink flew into the snow.

The producer yelled, "KEEP ROLLING!" like she was directing the season finale.

Brittany surfaced with a furious sputter, hair plastered to her cheeks, eyes blazing.

Jonah popped up right after her, grinning like the most dangerous kind of man: the quiet one who finally snapped.

Their faces were inches apart.

Steam curled around them.

The whole hot tub leaned in.

And Brittany, breathless and dripping, had never looked more alive.

"Jonah, we haven't seen each other since we were *kids.* What are you doing?"

Brittany hissed the words, breathless and dripping, her hand gripping the edge of the hot tub like it was the only stable surface left in her world.

Jonah didn't back off.

Not even an inch.

Water beaded down his jaw, catching in the stubble that was absolutely not there nine years ago, and his eyes locked on hers with an intensity that made her lungs forget their job.

"What I missed doing," he murmured, voice low and steady, "for nine years."

And then his hand slid to the back of her neck.

Gentle.

Sure.

Claiming.

He pulled her in.

Not a hesitation.

Not a question.

A kiss — right there, in front of the cameras, the contestants, the winter night, the producer having nineteen heart attacks out of frame.

And God help her...Brittany *wanted* it.

Her lips parted.

Her breath caught.

Every part of her leaned closer without thinking, without choosing, without permission.

It felt like something inevitable.

Like gravity.

Like memory and longing and unfinished business all braided into one terrifying, magnetic pull.

But then—Then reality slammed back in.

Her plan.

Her *degree.*

The reason she was here in the first place.

Brittany shoved off him with both feet planted squarely on his hips.

The push was powerful enough to send Jonah back a few inches, ripples bursting across the surface like firecrackers.

She spun toward W-Guy (whatever, he'd do fine as a prop).

"Piss off, Jonah," she snapped, flipping her drenched hair over her shoulder with weaponized precision. "You don't get to have this."

Her tone was cold.

Her eyes were not.

Jonah...Jonah just grinned wider.

Oh no.

OH NO.

He wasn't offended.

He was *interested.*

"We'll see, princess," he said softly, voice dipping into a lethal register.

Then, with a wicked tilt of his head—

"Or is it queen now?"

A beat.

A tremor in Brittany's chest.

Around them, the hot tub was silent.

Even the bubbles seemed to stop to eavesdrop.

Trevor's Sauna Confessional

The sauna was a glowing cedar box of ego and steam.

Trevor sat in the center, spread out like a king on a throne, glistening under the soft amber lights, his towel slung low to ensure maximum coverage on screen — and by coverage, he meant exposure.

Because Trevor always knew his angles.

Trevor *invented* his angles.

"Okay, we're rolling!" a PA called through the crack in the door.

Trevor flashed a smile so white it could cause snow blindness.

"Well," he began, leaning back like a man settling into his own legend, "Trevor is feeling good about the competition so far."

He folded his hands behind his head.

No microphone could fully capture the sound of his biceps flexing, but Trevor believed in miracles.

"Trevor's got options," he continued. "Trevor could honestly take any guy out first, but Jonah..." He paused, dramatic. "Jonah has main-character energy that offends Trevor on a spiritual level."

The camera operator coughed in agreement.

"But let's talk about Brittany," Trevor said, lowering his voice as if delivering a secret. "Trevor sees what she's doing. Trevor appreciates a woman who pretends to be unaffected by Trevor."

He tapped his chest lightly.

"Trevor knows she's not unaffected. No one is unaffected by Trevor."

He leaned forward now, elbows on his knees, confidence radiating like heat waves off asphalt.

He spread his hands.

"But listen — Trevor can handle a little competition."

Another grin, the kind that belonged in a cologne commercial.

"Trevor thinks Brittany needs someone who isn't scared of her villain era."

He shrugged, golden and smug.

"Lucky for her, Trevor thrives in chaos."

He held up a finger.

"Jonah's days? Numbered."

Trevor held up a second finger.

"Brittany? Hers for the taking. With me beside her."

He settled back again, utterly pleased with himself.

"Trevor out."

The PA whispered outside the door, reverently, "Cut."

For the Camera

The producer — finally introducing herself as Steph, clipboard hugged to her chest like a sacred relic — gathered the group on the snowy deck with the reverence of someone about to summon television magic.

"Okay, everyone," she said brightly, "here's how the rest of the night goes. I need flirting, hands on bare waists, two or three kisses, a little tension, a tiny fight — tiny! cute! — and then we wrap with gossip back in the dorms. Got it?"

The contestants nodded, some eager, some terrified, some already practicing their "natural" hair flips.

Steph clapped sharply.

"Places! And... ACTION!"

Trevor exploded into movement like a golden retriever who had heard the word "treat."

He practically *teleported* back into the hot tub, sliding into the spot beside Brittany with a confidence that would crumble lesser mortals.

"So, gorgeous," he purred, draping an arm behind her shoulders without touching her. "What are you going to do with the prize money?"

Brittany masked every real thought with a lazy, elegant shrug.

She wasn't about to tell anyone she wanted a social work degree.

Reality TV was a battlefield.

You didn't hand out your heart like free samples.

"Trip to Europe," she said lightly. "Maybe a car. You know... fun stuff."

Across the tub, one of the girls snorted — Brittany was pretty sure her name was Jan? Jayne? Something an attitude.

"A waste," Jan/Jayne declared, lifting her chin. "I'm going to use the money to go to Africa to build schools. And dig wells."

Her tone dripped with self-righteous purity, the kind that played well on Instagram reels and charity galas.

Trevor's brows shot up.

W blinked like he'd just been asked to solve algebra.

Brittany...Brittany smiled.

But it wasn't a nice smile.

She'd come in knowing exactly who she would be.

The villainess.

The ice queen.

The firecracker who made the audience yell at their screens and rewind scenes for the drama.

Villains outlasted the forgettable ones.

Villains earned edits.

Villains got invited back.

So she tilted her head just slightly, lashes half-lowered, a subtle sneer curling her mouth.

"Oh," she said, sweet and venomous at once. "You're one of those."

Jan/Jayne bristled instantly.

Brittany laughed — light, melodic, *devastating*.

Even the hot tub jets seemed to recoil.

Trevor stared at her like she'd just invented fire.

Jan/Jayne stormed into the sauna like the producers had personally offended her soul.

She sat down on the cedar bench with the grace of a woman who believed she was here for a charity campaign, not a dating experiment. Her towel was cinched too tight, her jaw even tighter, and the second the PA whispered "rolling," Jan/Jayne exploded.

"Okay, FIRST of all," she said, stabbing a finger toward the camera, "my name is Janessa. Not Jan. Not 'Jan?' with a question mark. And CERTAINLY not 'Hey, what's-your-name-again?' like everyone keeps saying."

She flung her hair over her shoulder in a deeply dramatic, deeply unflattering motion.

"I have BEEN here for four hours and somehow nobody knows who I am because *she—*."

She snatched up a piece of air, squeezing it like it was Brittany's throat.

"—Has hijacked every scene since she arrived."

Her nostrils flared.

"Brittany with a B? With a B like Bitch? REALLY? That's what we're doing?"

She mocked the pose: chin lifted, lips pursed, eyes narrowed in faux menace.

"That's SO TIRED. That's S O O O 2016. Oh wow, you're mean and pretty? What a REVOLUTIONARY CHARACTER ARC."

She shoved her hands into the air.

"And can we TALK about how I literally said I would use the prize money to build SCHOOLS and DIG WELLS in AFRICA and the cameras immediately swivelled to her like she'd just invented FIRE?"

She gasped, offended all over again.

"Are we SERIOUS? Is THAT what people want? They want... villains?!"

Her voice cracked into a pitch only dogs and producers could hear.

"I'm GOOD TV! People LOVE a humanitarian! They LOVE someone who wants to make the world better! I am VERY give-back-to-the-community coded!"

She slapped her chest for emphasis.

"I HAVE DEPTH!"

She threw up her hands.

"But nooo, everyone only sees Brittany. Brittany in the hot tub. Brittany laughing. Brittany flipping her hair. Brittany breathing oxygen like it's her THING."

She leaned forward, eyes wild.

"Well guess WHAT? Janessa is HERE. JANESSA IS A CONTESTANT. JANESSA HAS GOALS. JANESSA HAS A STORYLINE TOO!"

She pointed directly at the lens.

"And if they think I'm going to let some moody Arctic Barbie outshine me, they've got another thing coming."

The PA whispered, "...cut?"

Janessa flopped back dramatically.

"Finally."

Chocolate Milk

Night settled over the eco-lodge like velvet.

The northern lights flickered faintly—more teal than green—hovering behind the clouds like they were waiting for the drama to peak.

Steph called, "Everyone into natural connections mode!" which was production-speak for *go flirt with someone*, and *dear God give me usable footage*.

The contestants obeyed immediately.

Tyler and red-bikini Aaliyah got out of the hot tub, put on robes and boots and drifted toward the roaring firepit, laughing way too loudly.

Trevor swooped in on Janessa—Trevor had decided she was a "chaos magnet" and therefore great for screen time—while Janessa pretended she wasn't still fuming about Brittany's villain arc stealing her lighting.

W had somehow ended up sitting on the edge of the hot tub with different girl in his lap.

Hook-ups were already happening.

Production assistants were already whispering excitedly.

Cameras zoomed on hands under water like they were filming a documentary on mating rituals.

But Brittany?

Brittany had retreated to the shadowy corner of the hot tub, champagne flute perched delicately in her fingers, face perfectly neutral.

Ice queen activated.

She looked like she was carved from glaciers and good intentions burned to ash.

Until—

Jonah slid into the water beside her.

No hesitation.

No announcement.

Just the quiet displacement of water and the warmth of him taking up too much space, too close, too Jonah.

Brittany stiffened, nose lifting just a fraction.

"Don't," she warned. "Don't say whatever you came here to say."

Jonah rested an arm on the edge behind her, effectively caging her in without touching her.

He didn't look at the cameras.

He didn't look at the other contestants.

He only looked at her.

"You're doing the ice queen thing," he said softly.

"I *am* the ice queen thing," she shot back.

He smiled.

Warm.

Dangerous.

Nuclear.

"You weren't always."

Her jaw tightened.

"Jonah—"

"Remember when we snuck into Mr. Bennett's science class after hours?"

Her composure cracked.

Barely.

"We... that was a long time ago."

"You said we needed the microscope to check if a piece of your hair had split ends."

Brittany pressed her lips together, refusing to give him anything.

"You said it was 'urgent scientific exploration.'"

Her throat bobbed.

"And then," Jonah continued, voice dropping to something unbearably fond, "you knocked over a beaker and snorted chocolate milk out your nose."

Brittany inhaled sharply—

—right as she took a sip of champagne.

It shot out of her nose like a high-pressure fountain.

She slapped a hand to her face.

"Oh my GOD—Jonah!!"

Jonah was laughing so hard he had to grip the side of the tub.

Contestants stared.

Janessa whispered, horrified, "That is... so humanizing."

Trevor applauded.

Steph actually fist-pumped behind the monitor.

Brittany sputtered, mortified, watery-eyed, swatting his arm.

"I hate you," she gasped.

"No you don't," he said gently.

And the look he gave her wasn't teasing now.

It was history.

It was warmth.

It was something she'd spent nine years trying not to need.

Dorm Gossip

The Guys

The guys' dorm already smelled like damp towels, body spray, testosterone, and very poor life choices.

Steph's assistant, Paige, casually strolled in and said loudly:

"Steph wants natural conversation. Especially about Brittany."

She winked.

The men nodded like they had no idea they were being manipulated.

They absolutely did.

Josh crashed onto his bunk.

Tyler flexed unconsciously.

W (officially short-formed now) kept checking his reflection in his phone camera.

Trevor sat cross-legged in the center of the room like a cult leader.

"So," he began, rubbing his hands together, "Trevor thinks we should talk strategy."

Tyler grinned.

"About Brittany?"

Trevor pointed at him like *yes, my son, you get it.*

"Trevor saw the slap," Tyler continued. "You think that was real?"

Josh shook his head.

"No way. They know each other. Did you not see the way he looked at her? That's not stranger energy. That's... unresolved."

W leaned in.

"Bro, she flirted with me earlier."

Trevor patted his shoulder.

"No she didn't."

Josh laughed so hard he fell off the bunk.

Tyler crossed his arms.

"Well I want to know what happened between them."

Trevor nodded sagely.

"Trevor believes Jonah is the biggest competition. Trevor believes Brittany wants someone who can handle fire. Trevor also believes—"

Josh interrupted.

"You talk about yourself in third person a lot, bro."

Trevor gestured to his torso.

"When you look like this? You have to."

Josh sighed dramatically and flopped back onto his pillow.

"I'm just saying — when he pulled her under the water? That was... that was something."

The room went quiet.

Even Trevor nodded slowly, impressed.

"Trevor admits," he said solemnly, "that was a power move."

Josh lowered his voice.

"So does anyone know their history?"

They all shook their heads.

But every single one of them thought the same thing:

Jonah and Brittany weren't a TV storyline.

They were a detonation waiting to happen.

The Gals

Upstairs, the girls' dorm was a chaos nest of hairbrushes, lotion, pyjamas, and whispered screaming.

Steph herself popped her head in.

"Ladies," she sang sweetly, "talk about Jonah."

Then she shut the door. Hard.

The women pounced on the topic like starved raccoons on a donut.

Aaliyah sat cross-legged on the bed, brushing her hair.

"Okay, so, Jonah. Thoughts?"

The woman beside her — Kelsey — sighed dreamily.

"He's so quiet. But like... sexy quiet. Like he knows things."

A chorus of *yesssss* rippled around the bunk beds.

Another woman piped up, "Did you see the way he looked at Brittany? Like he'd seen a ghost but wanted to make out with the ghost?"

Aaliyah nodded enthusiastically.

"Oh absolutely. That's history. That's emotional baggage. That's trauma bonding waiting to happen."

Kelsey sighed.

"He's the kind of guy who remembers your favourite cookie."

Aaliyah leaned forward, conspiratorial.

"Did you notice how he got in the hot tub? No splash. Just... slide, like a panther."

Everyone moaned.

Janessa threw her pillow across the room.

"THIS IS RIDICULOUS. Why is everyone obsessed with him?!"

Aaliyah shrugged.

"Because he has mystery. And cheekbones. And arms."

The group murmured in deep agreement.

"And," Kelsey added softly, "because Brittany is the only girl he sees."

The room fell quiet.

Every single head slowly turned toward Brittany's empty bunk.

Someone whispered, "She's lucky."

Someone else whispered, "Or doomed."

Janessa huffed, "Well *I'm* not giving up."

Aaliyah smirked.

"Oh honey... nobody cares."

Confessionals

Jonah

The sauna door clicked shut behind him.

Jonah sat on the bench, elbows on his knees, towel slung low, water still dripping from his hair. The heat made everything hazy — or maybe that was just *her* still rattling around behind his ribs.

The PA whispered, "Rolling."

Jonah exhaled deeply.

"I didn't think I'd see her again," he said.

No theatrics.

Just raw truth.

He rubbed a hand over his face.

"Brittany was... she was my person. My—"

He cut himself off, jaw tightening.

He wasn't about to cry on national television.

"She disappeared," he finally managed. "One day she was just gone. No phone calls. No messages. Nothing. I didn't know if she was okay. I didn't know if she was alive. I didn't know—"

He swallowed.

"Anything."

He looked directly at the camera then.

"But when I walked in and saw her..."

His voice softened.

"You don't forget someone like Brittany. You don't forget the way she laughed in science class. Or the way she challenged you. Or the way she made you feel like you were... important."

He shook his head, half-smile tugging the corner of his mouth.

"She's different now. Tougher. Sharper. But she still does that thing where she pretends she's fine when she's absolutely not."

A slow, knowing grin spread across his face.

"And I'm not scared of her. Not then. Not now."

The PA mouthed: HOLY SHIT.

Steph, watching on a monitor, fanned herself with her clipboard like she needed medical attention.

Brittany

Brittany flopped into the sauna chair like a woman who had survived a war. She still smelled faintly of champagne, hot tub chemicals, and humiliation.

"Rolling!" called the PA.

Brittany forced a smile, then immediately dropped it.

"Let's get this over with," she muttered.

She crossed her arms tightly over her chest.

"So... Jonah."

A beat.

An eye roll.

"Look, we went to high school together. He was a friend. A *good* friend. Probably the best one I had. But that's ancient history. Doesn't matter now."

Her knee bobbed impatiently.

"And sure, he's... grown up. A lot. He looks... fine."

She looked away from the camera as she said it.

(He looked illegal, Brittany. ILLEGAL.)

"But whatever nostalgia he thinks we have? It was nine years ago. I don't know him anymore."

She uncrossed her legs, then recrossed them.

"The almost kiss? That wasn't— I mean, I wasn't actually going to kiss him. Obviously. It was TV. Drama. Whatever."

She waved a hand dismissively but her voice wobbled.

"And him bringing up that stupid science class incident? That was a low blow. An emotional cheap shot. Unfair. And rude. And—"

She pressed two fingers to her forehead.

"And he made me snort champagne. On camera."

She groaned, dropping her head back against the wall.

A whisper.

"I don't hate him."

Her eyes widened as she realized she said it out loud.

"CUT!" Steph yelled from the hallway, because she needed the footage but also because Brittany looked like she might spontaneously combust.

Steph's Strategy Meeting

Steph didn't sleep.

Producers rarely did, but tonight?

Tonight she didn't sleep because she was BUZZING.

She walked into the production control room at dawn, caffeine in one hand, clipboard in the other, already firing orders at the bleary-eyed crew like a general preparing for war.

"Okay people — we need to rethink the breakfast challenge."

Her assistant, Paige, blinked at her.

She slapped her clipboard on the desk.

"Do you know what we have? Do you know what JUST fell into our laps?"

The entire crew stared at her.

She stabbed her pen into the air like she was announcing the existence of a new star.

"A REAL LOVE STORY."

Half the room gasped.

The other half whispered reverently.

Steph began pacing like a mad scientist.

"Jonah and Brittany are GOLD. They're tension. They're unresolved. They're giving me *slow-burn-with-jealousy-overtones.* Do you understand how rare that is on episode one?!"

Paige nodded furiously.

"Ratings catnip."

"Exactly."

Steph spun back to the whiteboard and scribbled:

BREAKFAST CHALLENGE— Pairing MUST be Jonah + Brittany— Others: chaos filler

A camera operator frowned.

"But we told the contestants pairings were random. Won't they notice?"

Steph barked a laugh.

"They're tired. They're hungry. They're half hungover from 'champagne.' They'll notice nothing. Besides—" she pointed to a monitor showing Jonah and Brittany's confessionals side-by-side, *both* looking emotionally destroyed in totally different ways, "—if they DO notice? Even BETTER. More drama."

Paige raised a hand timidly.

"And the challenge itself?"

Steph grinned like she was plotting a coup.

"Something intimate. Something contact-heavy. Something where the other contestants have no choice but to WATCH."

Paige scribbled notes frantically.

"Also," Steph added, pacing again, "we need to keep Trevor AWAY from Brittany. He's pure chaos but the wrong kind — he'll derail the emotional payoff."

A tech muttered, "Trevor is very loud."

Everyone nodded in terrified unison.

She checked her watch.

"Breakfast in twenty."

Steph clapped once.

"Okay team, let's go make television history."

The Breakfast Challenge

The contestants filed into the lodge's great room, still rubbing sleep from their eyes, wrapped in blankets and steaming coffee cups. The long wooden table in the center had been cleared, replaced with padded mats and ominous-looking placards that read:

> BREAKFAST CHALLENGE
> NO HANDS.
> SEXY POINTS MATTER.

Brittany narrowed her eyes immediately.

Steph bounced to the front of the room like a woman who'd slept five hours in total the entire season and loved it.

"Okay everyone!" she chirped, clapping her hands. "Today's challenge is a *fun*, *flirty*, *interactive* moment for bonding!"

Trevor raised a hand.

"Is Trevor going to be oiled?"

Steph ignored him.

She gestured dramatically to the mats.

"Men, you're the tables. Lie back. Stay still. Look appealing."

A few guys immediately straightened their hair.

Trevor reclined like a Roman emperor mid-orgy.

"Ladies," Steph continued, "you will be eating breakfast off the male contestants with NO HANDS ALLOWED."

Silence.

Then utter pandemonium.

Tyler fist-pumped.

Aaliyah groaned, "God, my mother's watching this show."

Janessa looked physically ill.

But Brittany?

Brittany sniffed, unimpressed.

"Good thing I'm not hungry," she said dryly, folding her arms like a queen bored by mere mortals.

Steph's head whipped toward her so fast her ponytail cracked like a whip.

She snapped her fingers.

"Uh-uh. No. *Absolutely not.* If you don't eat, you lose. And if you lose, you get a penalty."

The room gasped.

Even Trevor straightened.

Brittany raised an eyebrow.

"A penalty? For not licking food off a man's torso? That feels vaguely litigious."

Steph grinned like a cat with a mouse-sized Emmy nomination.

"And—" she sang, "IF you participate... and if you and your partner are voted *sexiest* by your fellow contestants?"

She paused for maximum effect.

"You BOTH get immunity from elimination."

Brittany froze.

Immunity.

The holy grail.

The ultimate safety net.

The difference between staying long enough to secure tuition money... and washing out early.

Steph watched the shift happen behind Brittany's eyes and nodded like a proud mentor in a villain origin story.

"There she is," Steph whispered. "My girl."

Brittany glared.

But her jaw set with resolve.

"Fine," she said. "I'll play."

Jonah—already reclining on a mat, arms behind his head, looking far too smug—lifted an eyebrow.

"Good," he said. "Because I'm prepared."

The Table

The PAs descended like highly trained soldiers of chaos, carefully arranging food on the men's torsos with clinical precision. Tiny pancakes. Whipped cream squiggles. Strategically placed berries. One overly enthusiastic PA added a drizzle of maple syrup down Jonah's side abs "for sheen."

Jonah just muttered, "This feels sticky already."

Brittany rolled her eyes so hard she saw the northern lights behind them.

She moved into the kneeling position Steph demanded — the *"ooh let's pretend it's yoga but it's not"* kneel — hair tumbling over her shoulder, posture immaculate, expression WHOLLY unimpressed.

"This is not a thing," she hissed under her breath.

Jonah tilted his head toward her, the smuggest smirk alive on his gorgeous, infuriating face.

"Of course it's a thing," he murmured. "You're just mad you don't get to control the sitch."

Brittany's left eye twitched.

"No one says 'sitch' anymore."

Jonah's grin deepened.

"What can I say? I'm vintage."

She almost slapped him again.

Almost.

Steph clapped loudly.

"AND... ACTION!"

Across the room, Janessa immediately leapt into performance mode.

"Oh dear," she moaned theatrically, loud enough to echo, "what am *I* supposed to do with so much delicious food on such a scrumptious table?"

Every contestant within three meters cringed.

Brittany had to physically bite her lip to keep from laughing.

She felt Jonah's stomach shake beneath her — he was laughing too.

Steph yelled, "JANESSA, BACK TO CENTER. BOOBS TO CAMERA."

Janessa obeyed like she was being paid extra.

Brittany refocused.

Sexy, huh?

Fine.

If it was sexy the producers wanted...

Then Jonah was going to have a full body crisis.

She leaned over him, slow and deliberate, letting her hair spill like a curtain around them.

The air between them warmed. Jonah's breath hitched.

A single ripe strawberry rested on his navel, the most innocent fruit suddenly weaponized.

Brittany lowered her mouth close — so close he could feel her breath — and inhaled softly.

"I always love," she purred, voice low smoke and danger, "a nice ripe strawberry."

Jonah's eyes went feral.

Then she used her tongue — a teasing, slow scoop — to lift the berry.

Only... she fumbled it.

Instinct took over.

She snapped forward and caught it between her teeth — and in doing so, her lips brushed Jonah's stomach.

The sound Jonah made was NOT meant for broadcast.

A punched-out inhale, sharp and desperate.

His hands flexed uselessly at his sides — he wasn't allowed to move.

Torture.

Absolute torture.

Brittany looked up, berry between her teeth, and winked.

"Jo," she murmured, voice soft enough only he could hear, "we haven't even gotten to the good part yet."

Jonah groaned — a real, from-the-gut, unfiltered sound that sent the entire camera crew into silent, vibrating hysterics.

Steph clutched her clipboard like it was a life raft.

This was gold.

Absolute television gold.

If Jonah was in hell, it was the most sensual hell ever designed.

He forced himself to breathe evenly, eyes closed, muscles tight with restraint.

Steph had told the men to "look relaxed," but Jonah was about as relaxed as a live wire dropped in snowmelt.

Because Brittany was licking breakfast off him.

With a mouth he'd spent nine years *not* thinking about.

Except he *had* thought about it.

Too often.

And now every single repressed fantasy was slamming into him like a truck on a frozen highway.

He tried to meditate.

He tried to focus on his breathing.

He tried counting backwards from a thousand.

It did not help.

Because Brittany kept brushing against him — lips, breath, tongue — in soft, unintentional (and intentionally devastating) touches.

Meanwhile, on the other side of the room, Trevor was narrating like he was filming a National Geographic special.

"Well now, this is the rare Janessa in her natural habitat," Trevor intoned dramatically, as Janessa awkwardly bent over his abs. "Observe her rigid posture. Notice the way she attempts seduction with the enthusiasm of a tax auditor."

Janessa hissed, "TREVOR STOP TALKING."

Trevor ignored her.

"Here comes the moment," he whispered loudly. "Will the Janessa succeed in retrieving the syrup-drizzled blueberry WITHOUT using hands? Or will she perish under the weight of unrealistic expectations?"

Janessa lunged, face-planting into Trevor's sternum.

Trevor gasped theatrically.

"She attacks! She STRIKES!"

The crew lost it behind their cameras.

But none of that — none of the chaos, the noise, the laughter — mattered to Jonah.

Because Brittany was leaning in again, breath brushing the sensitive skin just below his ribs.

And that's when it slipped out.

"Brittany..."His voice was low, rough, ragged — gravel dragged over heat.

Barely audible over Trevor's nature documentary reenactment.

But Brittany felt it.

She *felt* it in her bones, in the back of her throat, in the way her breath stuttered.

She froze.

"Jonah... don't."

Barely a whisper.

Barely anything at all.

But the microphones heard it.

Oh, the microphones heard EVERYTHING.

And Steph?

Steph was offscreen doing an internal happy dance so violent it could've powered the entire lodge.

She mouthed at the audio tech:

"WE GOT IT. WE GOT THE MOMENT."

Brittany didn't dare look at Jonah now.

Because if she did...

She knew she'd break.

And Jonah?

Jonah lay there trembling — not from the cold, not from the cameras, but because her voice *still* did something to him.

Something dangerous.

The challenge wasn't over.

But they were.

The Vote

"AND—CUT!" Steph shouted, voice cracking with triumph. "Jesus Christ, that was art."

The second the word *cut* left her lips, Jonah sat up like someone had snapped a cord holding him underwater.

He dragged in a breath so sharp it punched the cold air around him.

He didn't look at Brittany.

Couldn't.

Because if he looked at her — disheveled hair, flushed cheeks, lips slightly parted from kissing breakfast off his skin — he was going to do something profoundly unwise.

Like grab her and kiss her until neither of them remembered the challenge, the cameras, the entire show, or their own damn names.

He raked a hand through his hair instead, chest rising and falling like he'd just escaped a predator.

Which...

He kind of had.

Brittany.

He was sweating, but it wasn't from the challenge.

Across the mat, Brittany shot to her feet so fast she nearly slipped.

She didn't look back.

She didn't trust a single muscle in her body.

She marched away on autopilot, head high, ponytail swaying, the picture of icy composure—

Except for the truth:

Her lips were buzzing.

Her stomach was flipping.

Her pulse was in open revolt.

She was seconds — literal seconds — from climbing Jonah like he was a six-foot-two tree made exclusively for cardio activities.

"Nope," she muttered under her breath.

"Nope nope nope."

She shook out her hands like that could dislodge whatever had just detonated inside her.

It didn't.

Behind her, Jonah watched her walk away with a look that could shatter glass.

He pressed the heel of his hand to his forehead.

What the hell were they doing?

Steph appeared behind a monitor whispering, "This isn't a show anymore. This is a RELIGION."

The contestants were herded back into the lodge's main room, still flushed, still damp, still trying to pretend they hadn't just turned a breakfast challenge into a televised panic attack.

Steph bounced in front of them with her clipboard like a caffeinated commander.

"Okay everyone! TIME TO VOTE for the *sexiest pair*."

The room buzzed.

Jonah looked straight at the floor.

Brittany looked straight at the ceiling.

Neither dared look at each other because eye contact would equal spontaneous combustion.

Steph passed out the tiny wooden voting tokens — cute, shaped like snowflakes, but emotionally? Weapons.

"Remember," she sang sweetly, "the winning pair gets IMMUNITY."

Trevor raised his hand.

"Yes, Trevor has a question: does Trevor get extra points for narration?"

"No," Steph replied flatly.

"Trevor disagrees."

Josh elbowed him.

"Dude, vote."

The voting bowls sat on a table, each labeled with pair names:

- *Jonah & Brittany*
- *Trevor & Janessa*
- *Tyler & Aaliyah*
- *Wade (finally) & Kelsey*
- *Others (Bless their hearts)*

One by one, contestants stepped forward.

Aaliyah dropped her token in Jonah & Brittany without hesitation.

"Sorry y'all, that was... cinematic."

Tyler followed.

"Oh yeah. That was like... rated R."

Trevor strutted up, placed his token in Trevor & Janessa, and patted the bowl lovingly.

"Trevor supports Trevor."

Janessa stomped up behind him and also dropped her vote in Trevor & Janessa, glaring at everyone like they were all personally sabotaging her charity tour.

Steph cleared her throat.

"Alright! Votes are in!"

She dramatically unscrewed the lids like she was opening ancient scrolls.

"Coming in third place..."

She revealed the card.

"Tyler & Aaliyah!"

Cheers.

"Second place..."

She paused for suspense.

"Trevor & Janessa!"

Trevor pumped both fists.

"Trevor accepts this honor."

Janessa beamed like she'd cured frostbite.

"And in FIRST place..."

Steph snapped open the last card.

"By a landslide..."

Her grin was feral now — pure producer ecstasy.

"JONAH. AND. BRITTANY."

The room ERUPTED.

Cheers, whistles, shocked laughter.

Jonah's head whipped up.

Brittany's jaw dropped.

Tyler yelled, "THE CHEMISTRY WAS CHEMISTRYING!"

Aaliyah screamed, "THE WAY HE GROANED??? COME ON."

Jonah turned to Brittany slowly, like looking too fast might break him.

She swallowed.

They both looked like people who had just been handed a prophecy they didn't ask for.

First Elimination

By the time lunch rolled around, everyone looked hungover from emotions rather than alcohol.

Puffy eyes. Suspiciously quiet chewing. The kind of stiff body language that said *someone cried in the shower and won't admit it.*

Except Jonah and Brittany.

They had immunity.

A shiny golden shield of safety.

Steph had arranged the dining room like it was a high-end brunch restaurant: fluffy omelettes, smoked salmon, stacks of pastries, fruit towers, and a level of presentation that said *"this is going to be immediately ruined by drama."*

Brittany sat beside Jonah, fully aware that every contestant was side-eyeing them like they'd manifested a showmance overnight.

Jonah leaned back casually, one hand wrapped around a mug of coffee like he was posing for a lumberjack calendar.

"Feeling ready?" he murmured.

"For lunch? Yes," Brittany deadpanned. "For whatever nonsense Steph has planned? Never."

Steph banged a spoon against a champagne glass, practically glowing.

"GOOD MORNING, LOVERS AND LOSERS!"

A few contestants actually flinched.

"Time for our FIRST elimination," she announced with the glee of a woman about to watch fireworks detonate inside a dishwasher.

A collective groan rose through the room.

"You all know the rules," Steph continued. "Musical chairs. Four couples. Three spots. One couple goes home."

Jonah leaned toward Brittany, voice low. "At least we can't get eliminated."

She hissed under her breath, "Don't jinx it—this show violates so many of its own standards I wouldn't be surprised."

But sure enough, the PAs wheeled out a ridiculous circle of chairs—with velvet cushions and little brass plates like they'd been stolen from an opera house.

The music began.

The contestants circled.

Steph looked like she was conducting an orchestra of fear.

Trevor strutted around the chairs like a man on a catwalk. Janessa followed closely behind him, whispering, "Don't you dare trip, Trevor. I'm wearing lip gloss."

Trevor tossed his hair. "Trevor floats like a swan. Trevor does not trip."

He immediately tripped.

Janessa shrieked.

The music stopped.

Chaos broke out as couples dove, lunged, slammed down into chairs like they were fighting for survival in the Hunger Games: Northern Edition.

When the dust settled?

Tyler and Michelle (???) were standing chairless.

Molly —or Marcie? Mona? Something with a M—covered her face dramatically. Tyler bowed like he'd just lost a fencing match.

Everyone gasped in unison. A polite, fake gasp. The kind used at funerals for people you didn't actually know.

Aaliyah whispered loudly, "I'm so sad for—um—her... what's her name?"

Brittany leaned toward Jonah. "Molly?"

"Marcie."

"Mona?"

He shrugged helplessly. "She never introduced herself to me."

Steph stepped forward, clapping her hands sympathetically.

"Oh noooo! How tragic! How emotionally devastating for the narrative!"

It was absolutely none of those things.

Because Tyler had done nothing but flex. And M had said maybe eight words since arriving.

Still, they hugged everyone goodbye like they were leaving a long-running sitcom. Trevor even patted Tyler's shoulder.

"Trevor hopes your post-show job prospers."

Tyler blinked. "I'm a firefighter."

"Trevor stands by his statement."

Brittany sipped her coffee, amused.

"This is awful," she said.

Jonah gave her a sideways grin. "You're enjoying this."

"Of course I am. We're immune. It's the only time being cruel is socially acceptable."

He huffed a laugh, warmth flickering in his eyes.

As Tyler and M walked out into the snowy morning, the contestants clapped half-heartedly, Steph looked thrilled, and Jonah leaned in just slightly—just enough for Brittany to feel the brush of his shoulder.

"You ready for whatever comes next?" he asked.

She didn't answer.

Because her heart had already decided.

And she definitely wasn't ready for that.

Janessa's Sabotage Plot

The moment the immunity announcement ended, Janessa stormed off down the hall like a woman whose every dream had been personally stepped on by a pair of delicious, emotionally-damaged high-school-sweethearts-turned-reality-TV-lovers.

She burst into the girls' dorm, slamming the door behind her.

Kelsey looked up mid-mascara.

"...you good?"

"NO, I AM NOT GOOD."

Janessa paced, arms flailing, hair bouncing aggressively.

"DO YOU KNOW WHAT JUST HAPPENED?" she shrieked.

Aaliyah deadpanned, "Yes. The right couple won."

Janessa pointed a shaking finger at her.

"YOU TAKE THAT BACK."

Aaliyah went back to blending eyeshadow.

Janessa huffed and kept pacing.

"They think they're cute," she snarled. "They think they're some epic love story. They think they're unstoppable."

Kelsey: "Pretty much, yeah."

Janessa stopped.

Mouth twisted.

Eyes glinting.

"No."

She whispered it like a threat.

"No, no, NO."

She jabbed a finger in the air.

"I will NOT be overshadowed by Brittany-with-a-B. Not after all the work I've done. Not after the Africa thing. NOT AFTER THERE WAS SYRUP IN MY HAIR."

Aaliyah: "That was your choice, babe."

Janessa ignored her entirely.

"Oh she wants to play ice queen? Fine. Let her. Because I," she clutched her chest dramatically, "am about to start my OWN story arc."

Kelsey blinked.

"...a villain arc?"

Janessa smiled.

Not sweetly.

Not gently.

Slowly.

Sharply.

Like someone who had chosen evil with intention.

"Exactly."

She looked toward the hallway where Jonah and Brittany were being swarmed by cameras.

"I'm done being forgettable. I'm done being 'Jan?' with a question mark. They want drama?"

Her eyes gleamed.

"I'll give them drama."

Post-Vote Confessional

Jonah

Jonah dropped onto the sauna bench like gravity suddenly got personal.

The door shut.

The PA whispered, "Rolling."

And Jonah exhaled — long, shaky, like the last hour had aged him a decade.

He scrubbed a hand over his face.

"I didn't expect that," he said softly.

His voice cracked — just enough that the audio tech looked up sharply.

"I mean, I knew today was... weird. And intense. And..." He broke off, staring at the floor.

"And then they voted for us," he murmured. "Just like that. Like everyone else saw it."

Saw *them*.

He swallowed hard.

"Brittany didn't even look at me after the challenge. She just... left."

He gave a humorless laugh.

"Classic Brittany. Run first, think later."

He leaned back, towel sliding a little, chest rising and falling in uneven waves.

"She looked incredible," he admitted. "Not just— not like that. I mean she looked like herself."

His fingers tapped lightly on his knee.

"The way she used to look when she'd argue with teachers. Or tell me my hair looked stupid. Or—"

He pressed his lips together, eyes unfocused.

"Seeing her again..."

He breathed out.

"It felt like something that was missing came back. All at once. Too fast."

A long pause.

Then, hushed:

"And it scares the hell out of me."

The PA mouthed *"holy shit"* to Steph.

Steph whispered back, "CUT NOTHING. KEEP EVERYTHING."

Brittany

Brittany sat down in the sauna chair like it personally offended her.

Her lipstick half-worn, her pulse *definitely* not calm.

She glared at the camera.

"Let's get this over with," she snapped.

The PA cleared his throat.

"...Rolling."

Brittany crossed her legs, arms, emotions — everything she could possibly cross.

"So. Immunity."

She flicked her fingers in the air.

"Cool. Great. Whatever."

She did NOT sound cool.

Or great.

Or whatever.

She sounded like a raccoon trying to pretend it hadn't been caught stealing snacks.

"I mean, of COURSE we won," she added. "I'm competitive. Jo's... Jonah. Fine. Whatever."

She waved her hand again, this time more violently.

"It wasn't *sexy.* It was strategy. It was a challenge. I did what I had to do."

The camera zoomed in just as her cheeks flushed.

"And the... the strawberry thing was— look, things happen, okay? It was slippery. The lighting was bad. People were yelling 'no hands.' Nobody's to blame."

A beat.

She shut her eyes, mortified.

"Ugh, okay—FINE. It was a *little* sexy."

She pointed at the camera like it had personally betrayed her.

"But Jonah started it. He said my name like— like—"

She stopped.

Her throat worked around the words.

Her voice dropped to a whisper.

"Like he used to."

Her jaw clenched.

"And I don't... I can't..."She rubbed her forehead, exasperated.

"This is stupid. I'm here to win. I'm here for school. I'm not here for—"

She paused.

Her eyes softened — just for one split, unguarded moment.

"I'm not here for heartbreak again."

A quiet beat.

"Cut," Steph whispered, voice shaking because she knew she had gold.

A Moment

Jonah couldn't stay in the dorm another second.

The laughter, the bragging, Trevor reenacting Janessa falling onto his chest like a wounded falcon — none of it registered.

He needed to find her.

His feet moved on instinct, down the hallway, around the corner, past the window where the Arctic dawn was just barely bleeding blue over the snowfields.

He found her by the back deck, standing alone in the cold, arms wrapped tightly around herself.

Her breath came out in small, shaky puffs.

He stopped just a few steps behind her.

She didn't turn, but he saw her shoulders stiffen.

"Britt," he said quietly.

Just her name.

Soft, like a plea.

Her inhale stuttered.

Jonah swallowed hard.

His pulse hammered in his throat.

"It's been almost a decade," he said.

His voice was low, rough.

Truth scraped raw.

Brittany still didn't face him.

But her head dipped.

Just slightly.

Jonah stepped closer—not touching, just near enough that their reflections trembled together in the frost-streaked glass.

"I remember the day your mom died," he said. "And then you were gone. Before the funeral. Before anyone could even... say anything."

His breath fogged between them.

"I had this whole speech," he added, voice catching. "About how I was there. That you didn't have to go through it by yourself. And then—"

He let out a broken laugh.

"Then you were just... gone."

Her shoulders rose and fell once.

A ghost of a breath.

A ghost of a memory.

Jonah closed his eyes.

"That night," he whispered. "Before everything fell apart..."

He paused.

Chose honesty.

"...we had a moment."

The word wasn't big enough.

It wasn't close to big enough.

But it was all he could get out without his voice breaking.

"We held onto each other because everything hurt and nothing made sense and you were the only person who ever—"

His jaw tightened.

He forced the words out anyway.

"I've thought about that night for nine years."

A beat.

Maybe two.

"Have you?"

Brittany finally turned her head, just enough that he saw her profile — her lashes fluttering, her lips parted, her eyes shining with something she would absolutely deny later.

Her voice came quiet, small, a tremor in cold air.

"Jonah... don't."

Which wasn't an answer.

But it was.

Glitter Hurricane

Jonah took one slow, careful step toward Brittany.

Just one.

It wasn't much — barely a whisper of movement — but the world seemed to inhale with him.

His eyes locked on hers, the air between them thin and warm and charged—

And then the door SLAMMED open.

Like, violently.

Like someone trying to break into a Black Friday sale.

Janessa barrelled onto the deck like a glittered-up hurricane.

"Oh my GOOOOOD," she shrieked, dramatic hand to her chest. "Was that you? Was that your voice? Did you just *say her name* like that?!"

Jonah blinked, startled.

"Janessa—?"

She launched herself at him with the force of a misguided cannonball.

"I FELT MYSELF GO ALL SQUISHY," she declared, arms wrapping around him like she was trying to climb him. "You said 'Britt' in that gravelly voice and Trevor was RIGHT — you are VERY PANTHER-CODED."

Jonah stumbled backward, desperately trying not to grip her shoulders too hard while attempting to pry her off gently.

"Janessa, I—could you—hold on—"

But she wasn't listening.

Not even a little.

Jonah froze.

So did time.

So did the northern lights.

Across from them, Brittany's face went white, then red, then something Jonah couldn't name.

But she was already stepping back.

Already retreating.

Already pulling her walls up so fast they practically shattered the air.

"Britt—wait—" Jonah reached toward her, but Janessa was still clinging to him like a cartoon koala.

Too late.

Brittany spun on her heel and slipped into the shadows of the hallway, disappearing as fast as she had nine years ago.

Jonah sagged, defeated.

Janessa squeezed tighter.

"Don't worry," she cooed, "you'll get over her."

He closed his eyes.

"I won't."

Steph's camera crew behind the snowbank nearly passed out.

Trevor had been leaning casually against the end of the hallway, sipping a protein shake like he was watching a live wildlife documentary.

He wasn't supposed to be there.

He *knew* he wasn't supposed to be there.

That's why he was there.

From his vantage point, he saw everything:

- Jonah stepping toward Brittany like a man approaching his destiny

- Brittany looking like she was about to either cry or kiss him
- Janessa launching herself like a sparkly missile
- Jonah being physically tackled by pure delusion
- Brittany vanishing like mist in the morning sun

Trevor took one slow sip of his shake.

"Trevor senses turbulence," he murmured to himself.

A PA walking by froze."...what?"

Trevor set the shake down like a sacred object.

"Trevor has seen this before," he said gravely. "In the mating grounds of Maui. A male approaches a female—energy, longing, hair fluttering—and then a rogue third party barrels in and destroys the ecosystem."

The PA stared."...are you doing the nature documentary thing again?"

Trevor nodded solemnly.

"Trevor must narrate emotional carnage. It is in Trevor's DNA."

He folded his arms.

He nodded toward the hallway where Jonah had retreated, stiff and devastated.

"And THAT..." Trevor whispered, voice hushed with awe, "was a man who has experienced romantic whiplash severe enough to cause spinal injury."

The PA blinked."...you okay, dude?"

Trevor placed a gentle hand on his shoulder.

"Trevor has never been better."

Steph's Damage Control

Meanwhile, down in the production den, Steph was pacing so aggressively she was in danger of wearing a trench into the lodge floor.

Her assistant Paige trailed her nervously, clutching a stack of emergency forms.

"Okay," Steph said, half panicking, half euphoric. "We have a SITUATION."

Paige nodded.

"Yes. Yes. Janessa launched herself at Jonah like a rabid bat."

Steph pointed wildly at the large monitor still replaying the footage.

"LOOK AT THIS! This is a love story being tackled by a walking charity press release!"

Paige squinted.

"She's definitely going to sue us if she gets rejected on camera."

Steph flapped a hand.

"Oh please, she WANTS to be rejected on camera. It's the closest she's come to a plotline."

She spun around, eyes blazing.

"We CANNOT let Janessa torpedo the emotional arc. Jonah and Brittany are our entire season. They are the ratings. They are the storyline. They are the REASON Frost-Byte+ has the budget for the underwater drone."

Paige scribbled furiously on her clipboard.

"Okay, so what are we doing?"

"Damage control. Emergency intervention. Romance CPR."

Steph clapped her hands sharply.

"Plan A: Separate Janessa from Jonah at ALL times unless he requests it. Plan B: Jonah and Brittany need alone time—but not TOO alone time. Soft lighting. Confessionally lighting. Maybe a fireplace?"

Paige wrote:

<u>JANESSA SEPARATION PROTOCOL</u>

<u>FORCED PROXIMITY, B RATED</u>

"Janessa – something to distract her from Jonah."

Paige paused."...like what?"

Steph blew out a breath.

"I don't know. Something low-stakes where she can't injure herself or anyone else."

Paige scribbled:

<u>JANESSA: OCCUPY WITH TASKS</u>

Steph stopped pacing.

Breathed.

And then whispered, reverently:

"But oh my God... the footage."

She pressed a hand to her heart.

"That whisper. That tension. Brittany literally walking away in heartbreak. Jonah melting like butter under a heat lamp."

She turned to Paige with wild, unhinged eyes.

"This is a BAFTA-level love arc, Paige."

Paige nodded solemnly.

"A masterpiece."

Steph grinned.

"And I will NOT let Janessa ruin it."

Steph stood over the whiteboard like a general preparing to invade a small country with nothing but spreadsheets and spite.

"Okay team," she said, tapping her pen. "Janessa just detonated a whole scene. Brittany fled. Jonah is basically grieving a still-alive person. We need to FIX THIS."

Paige nodded, eyes wide.

"And by fix," Steph clarified, "I mean exploit gently for emotional truth."

The entire production team nodded reverently.

Steph slammed a new sticky note onto the board.

CHALLENGE #3'ARCTIC RESCUE SCENARIO'*(pairs must share a survival shelter)*

Paige blinked. "Isn't that the challenge where—"

"Yes," Steph said. "The one where they build a tiny emergency warmth tent and have to sit inside it... touching."

Paige squinted. "Like... touching touching?"

Steph grinned wickedly.

"YES, Paige. SHARED BODY HEAT. A romance classic. I didn't create this trope but I WILL perfect it."

She spun to the rest of the team.

"Pairings will be COMPLETELY RANDOM—" *air quotes so aggressive the lights flickered,* "—and also absolutely rigged so Brittany and Jonah end up in the same shelter."

A camera op raised a timid hand.

"What about Janessa?"

Steph didn't even blink.

"She gets Trevor."

Paige gasped. "Is that safe?"

"Emotionally? No," Steph said. "But narratively? It's GOLD."

She scribbled another note:

JANESSA DISTRACTION TASK:

Trevor, Keep Her Occupied

"Okay team," Steph announced, clapping her hands, "we're forcing Jonah and Brittany into a metaphorical and literal tent of reconciliation."

She pointed dramatically toward the doorway.

"LET. THERE. BE. ROMANCE."

Trevor Gives Brittany 'Advice'

Brittany had escaped to the lounge area, curling up on a couch like she could camouflage herself among throw pillows.

She was still rattled, still pissed, still embarrassingly... breathless.

Trevor plopped himself down across from her with the grace of a Labrador wearing rollerblades.

"Trevor has words," he said, hands steepled like a monk.

Brittany groaned. "Please no."

Trevor ignored her.

"Trevor saw the scene," he began solemnly. "Trevor sensed emotions so raw they could be lightly seared."

Brittany covered her face. "God, please shut up."

Trevor leaned closer, whispering like he was about to deliver ancient wisdom.

"Trevor believes you are in trouble."

Brittany froze like a startled deer.

"No I'm not," she snapped. "I'm not. I'm here to win and then leave, I'm not—"

Trevor held up a hand.

"When Jonah said 'Britt' in That Voice—"

"Stop saying 'That Voice.'"

"—in That Voice," Trevor repeated, louder, "your soul left your body. Trevor saw it."

Brittany threw a couch pillow at him.

He caught it with one hand like a smug golden retriever.

"Trevor also believes," he continued, "that when you walked away, Jonah's heart fell through the floor and into the Arctic permafrost."

Brittany glared. "Why are you like this?"

"Trevor feels deeply," he said simply.

"No you don't."

Trevor placed a dramatic hand over his heart.

"Trevor feels EVERYTHING."

She stared at him, exhausted.

"Are you giving me advice or are you trying to create content?"

Trevor nodded thoughtfully.

"Both. Trevor is a multi-purpose instrument."

She sighed.

He leaned closer.

"You love him," Trevor said softly.

She looked away.

Trevor grinned.

She picked up another pillow.

"Trevor believes you shouldn't throw—"

He got hit square in the face.

"—pillows," he finished, muffled.

The Rigged Short-Straw Pull

The contestants gathered in a semicircle outside the lodge, bundled in stylish Arctic gear that none of them were emotionally prepared for.

Steph stood in the middle holding a wooden box filled with *colour matching straws* that were absolutely, definitely, totally rigged.

She shook the box dramatically.

"Okay team!" she chirped. "Pairs for today's Arctic Hike Challenge will be chosen RANDOMLY."

Trevor whispered to a PA, "Trevor smells lies."

Steph glared at him.

"DRAW," she commanded.

One by one, contestants reached in.

Tyler pulled a straw and immediately grinned at Aaliyah.

Trevor pulled his straw, looked at Janessa, and visibly reconsidered his entire life path.

Then Brittany stepped forward.

She reached in, rolled her eyes, grabbed a straw...

Steph's smile was predatory.

Jonah stepped up.

He reached in calmly, like he already knew the outcome.

When he pulled his matching straw, his eyes flicked to Brittany's.

Matching colors.

Matching doom.

Brittany's throat bobbed.

Jonah's breath caught.

Trevor gasped loudly.

"Trevor senses destiny!"

Janessa threw her straw on the ground.

"ARE YOU SERIOUS?!"

Steph clapped her hands.

"Pair #1: Jonah and Brittany! The rest of you? Great, whatever, let's go!"

They set off in their groups, the snow crunching beneath their boots, the sun low enough that everything glowed gold.

Brittany and Jonah walked ahead, a few steps apart.

He kept trying to match her pace.

She kept speeding up to avoid it.

"So we're really doing this?" she muttered.

"Looks like it," Jonah said, voice steady even though his heart was doing gymnastics.

"You okay with that?"

He almost laughed.

"I prefer it," he said softly.

They hiked for 2 hours — past frozen lakes, icy ridges, fields of untouched snow.

Finally, as twilight streaked violet across the sky, they arrived at a wide clearing.

And it was stunning.

A bonfire crackled in the middle.

Tablecloth-covered wood planks held trays of catered steaming food—salmon, Bannock, spiced potatoes, roasted vegetables.

And overhead?

Faint wisps of green beginning to shimmer across the sky.

Even Brittany stopped walking.

"Oh," she whispered. "Wow."

Jonah watched her face instead of the sky.

Steph whispered to Paige, "Get the camera on Jonah's eyes—NOW."

They ate around the fire—quiet, warm, flickering light dancing across their faces.

Brittany tried not to notice how Jonah kept offering her the warmest spot near the flames.

Jonah tried not to notice how Brittany kept tucking her hair behind her ear whenever she was nervous.

Neither succeeded.

After dinner, Steph clapped loudly, startling literally every contestant.

"OKAY EVERYONE!" she shouted. "Time for the FINAL phase of the challenge!"

She gestured grandly to a pile of tiny rolled-up shelters and equipment bags.

"Each pair must set up their *survival tent* in the dark using ONLY your headlamps and teamwork!"

Aaliyah squinted at the tents.

"These are...small."

Steph smiled brightly.

"Oh, they're VERY small. Cozy, even."

Jonah stared at the kit.

"...this looks barely big enough for one person."

Steph beamed.

"Exactly."

Brittany choked.

"You're kidding."

"Nope!" Steph said. "Use the air mattress and the sleeping bag provided! Share warmth! Survive the night! Cute!"

She handed Jonah and Brittany their kit.

Jonah swallowed.

Brittany was expressionless, but her ears were turning pink.

Janessa wailed, "WHY AM I WITH TREVOR???"

Trevor hugged the tent kit to his chest.

"Trevor is honoured to protect you."

Janessa screamed into the void.

As the groups began fumbling through the darkness, Jonah clicked on his headlamp.

He glanced at Brittany.

"You ready?" he asked softly.

She blew out a breath.

"No," she said honestly.

He nodded.

"Me neither."

They knelt in the snow together.

Their hands brushed.

The tiny shelter, the cold, the night, the northern lights crackling overhead —

They were about to be trapped together.

All night.

In one sleeping bag.

Steph whispered behind the monitors, "THIS IS GOD-TIER TELEVISION."

Body Heat

Brittany was *convinced* Steph was taking notes straight from the Devil's personal suggestion box.

A tiny one-person tent?

One sleeping bag?

Share your body heat, children?

Absolutely satanic.

And worse?

She had nothing to say to Jonah.

Nothing real.

Nothing that didn't feel like peeling open a wound she'd stapled shut years ago.

As she knelt in the snow beside him, wrestling with an instruction manual written by trolls, her thoughts wouldn't stop.

What could she even say?

"Hey Jonah, sorry I blamed you for not coming after me even though you didn't know where I went, and that it isn't anyone's fault? But your family had resources and I wanted you to rescue me..."

Her throat tightened.

Another thought pushed in, quieter, bleeding:

We had something... and then I lost you too.

Her breath fogged in front of her face.

Jonah looked up at her just then and her entire insides lurched.

He looked like he wanted to say something too.

He didn't.

He kept tying the *stupid* guy-line on the *stupid* Satan-tent with those *stupid* strong hands she used to know.

Steph, watching in the monitors, fanned herself like she was overheating.

Brittany forced herself to focus on the plastic pole in her hands.

It snapped into place with a click that echoed louder than it should have in her chest.

She wasn't mad at Jonah anymore.

She was mad at fate.

At grief.

At *herself.*

And at how much she still wanted something she had no right wanting.

Jonah brushed her glove as they both reached for the same clip.

She flinched.

He froze.

For one endless, breathless second, they were suspended there—touching, not touching, drowning in everything unsaid.

Then she pulled back sharply, her voice too tight.

"Steph is actually inspired by Satan," she muttered.

Jonah huffed a laugh — soft, aching.

"I know," he said quietly. "But we have to get through the night somehow."

She swallowed.

Yeah.

That was the problem.

She wasn't convinced she would *survive* it.

The tent was like airplane-bathroom tiny.

Like "this was designed by someone who hates happiness" tiny. They had to shuck their outdoor gear before getting in, stripped down to their thermals in order to fit.

They slid into the single sleeping bag with all the grace of two raccoons trying to share a hoodie. Brittany kept her back to him, shoulders rigid, every muscle shouting *don't touch me, don't touch me, don't care at all, don't care even a little bit.*

Except... the bag didn't zip unless Jonah curved around her.

So he did.

Slowly.

Respectfully.

Carefully, like she was made of glass and dynamite.

His chest pressed to her spine, warmth radiating through layers that suddenly felt like nothing.

Her breath caught as his arm settled around her waist, not grabbing, not holding — just there because the bag demanded it.

His breath brushed her neck.

A soft exhale.

Warm.

Dangerous.

"At least now you can't run away," he murmured.

The joke was quiet.

Gentle.

Wary.

It landed anyway.

Brittany let out the smallest huff of a laugh — like her heart slipped and accidentally touched his for a second.

"Yeah," she whispered, "well. I don't want to talk though. There's nothing to say, Jonah."

There it was.

The shut door.

The wall.

The ice queen cloak slipping back into place.

He nodded behind her, his chin brushing her shoulder.

"Okay," he said softly. "Then... can **I** just say one thing?"

She didn't answer.

He lowered his voice until it threaded right into her bloodstream.

"I missed you."

She went still.

Completely, utterly still.

Then her inhale quivered.

And slowly… painfully… she relaxed against him, like her body decided the truth before her brain could protest.

Her voice was tiny when it came.

"I missed you too."

He closed his eyes.

She swallowed.

Hard.

"I didn't even get a chance to say goodbye," she whispered, each word cracking like thin ice. "They just showed up that morning. Made me pack a bag. No warning, no time. Next thing I knew I was on a plane to Argentina."

Her breath shuddered.

"I lost everything that day."

Jonah's arm tightened around her — just a fraction, just enough that she felt grounded instead of drifting.

"Not everything," he said quietly.

"You still had me."

She almost broke.

Almost.

"We were just kids, Jonah," Brittany whispered, her voice thin as cold air. "It was a bad time in my life, and you were there. If I'd stayed… we probably would've broken up in a day."

Jonah's arm tightened instinctively around her waist — not possessive, not demanding, just this helpless, aching reflex he couldn't stop.

"That's not true," he murmured.

His breath warmed the back of her neck.

"And you know it."

She squeezed her eyes shut.

"We loved each other," he whispered, soft but devastating. "We just didn't know it yet."

Her entire body went rigid.

Love.

The forbidden word.

The word she'd buried under continents and years and oceans.

Brittany's throat closed around a sob she refused to let out.

"Jonah," she managed, voice cracking, "it wasn't love."

A lie. A shield. A lifeline.

"It was grief," she pushed on, each word hurting more than the last. "And proximity. And hormones. And chaos."

She swallowed hard.

"You just... got that confused."

There was a silence so deep it felt like the air itself froze.

Jonah didn't pull away.

He didn't loosen his arm.

But she felt him go still.

Not angry.

Not hurt.

Just... winded.

Like she'd punched the breath out of him without meaning to.

After a long moment, he exhaled — shaky, quiet, wrecked.

"Grief and proximity," he repeated softly, a sad little almost-laugh in his voice. "Sure, Britt."

His forehead rested between her shoulder blades, defeated.

"But I think you're lying to yourself harder than you're lying to me."

Her eyes blurred.

Because damn him —he wasn't wrong.

Noises in the Night

For a few long breaths, the tent was silent.

Heavy.

Tense.

Two heartbeats pretending not to listen to each other.

Then—Somewhere across the campsite—

A tent erupted in unmistakable rhythmic moans, breathy gasps, and someone aggressively whisper-yelling, "Quiet! The mic is on!"

Brittany lost it.

She giggled.

Just a tiny one.

Just a breathy little *huh* of disbelief and amusement.

But she was spooned against Jonah, full body, no space at all between them...

...and that giggle made her whole body shake against his.

Jonah reacted.

Oh, he reacted.

And Brittany *felt it*.

Immediately.

Directly.

Intimately.

She went completely still.

"Oh," she whispered, eyes wide in the dark.

Jonah inhaled sharply behind her—a deep, shaky sound that hit her spine like a lightning strike.

"Sorry, Britt," he murmured, voice low and hoarse, as if dragged out of him.

"You've always..."

He swallowed.

"You've always done things to me."

Her breath caught.

He continued, barely a whisper.

"Especially that laugh."

The air between them thickened, charged, electric.

Warmth pooled low in her stomach, confusing and terrifying and familiar all at once.

She shouldn't feel this. She *couldn't* feel this.

But God, she felt everything.

Her pulse thrummed.

Her skin tingled where his breath touched her neck.

Her thighs pressed together involuntarily.

"Jonah..." she breathed, warning or plea, she didn't know.

He didn't move.

Didn't push.

Didn't even shift his hips away.

He just held her gently, like she was a memory he was afraid to break.

Brittany couldn't breathe.

Well, she *could*, but every inhale was Jonah.

Jonah's warmth.

Jonah's scent.

Jonah's everything.

Turning in the sleeping bag was supposed to give them space.

It absolutely did not.

Instead, she ended up chest-to-chest with him, so close their breaths mingled, so close she could see the silhouette of his jaw in the faint glow of the tent fabric.

So close her leg accidentally slid against his—

Oh god.

Why was he this warm?

Why did he still smell like home?

Like warmth and winter and something so heartbreakingly Jonah that it made her throat close.

Her face landed practically *in* his neck, brushing his pulse.

His hand automatically steadied her waist.

Her heart tried to body-slam its way out of her chest.

"Okay," she whispered, trying for rationality and failing miserably. "I'm thinking it would be better to—"

She didn't get to finish.

Because from two tents over came—

"OH—OH GOD—YES—YES—KEEP—YES—"

A sound so loud it should've come with a parental advisory sticker.

Brittany's eyes flew wide.

Then shot straight up to Jonah's.

For a half-second they were frozen, suspended between horror and hilarity.

Then—

They both broke.

Laughing.

Not quiet laughter.

Not cute laughter.

Not composed laughter.

No, this was full-body, shaking, gasping, *we are losing it at midnight in a tent in the Arctic* laughter.

Jonah buried his face in her shoulder, shoulders trembling, trying and failing to smother the sound.

Brittany laughed into his chest, fists curling into the front of his jacket because she couldn't hold herself up.

The tent shook with how hard Jonah was laughing.

Her breathless giggles tangled with his warmth until she couldn't tell which was hers and which was his.

"God," she wheezed, "you cannot make that sound right now—"

Another very enthusiastic "YES—OH—YES—YES!" echoed across the clearing.

Which somehow made it worse.

They collapsed into each other all over again.

Their noses brushed.

Their foreheads almost touched.

Their lips were dangerously, stupidly close.

And suddenly the laughter...softened.

Warmth simmered beneath it.

A flicker of something old and familiar and reckless sparked between them.

Brittany swallowed, heartbeat thundering.

"Okay," Jonah whispered, breath ghosting her lips, "now what were you saying?"

She couldn't remember a single word.

Almost

For one suspended, impossible moment—time stopped.

The world shrank to the glow of the lantern outside, the rustle of the sleeping bag, the warmth of Jonah's breath brushing her lips.

Brittany leaned in first.

Slowly.

Hesitantly.

Like a woman who knew she shouldn't but physically could no longer obey her own rules.

Her fingers curled in the fabric of his thermal shirt.

Her heartbeat punched at her ribs.

Her face tilted up—

Their lips brushed.

Not a kiss.

Not yet.

Just a soft, trembling, agonizing graze that felt like memory and longing and nine years of swallowed feelings snapping free.

Jonah's breath stopped.

His hand slid up the curve of her waist.

He angled closer—

And then—

"TREVOR! STOP SNORING OR I WILL SMOTHER YOU IN YOUR SLEEP!"

Janessa's voice ripped through the campsite like the shriek of a vengeful polar goddess.

Brittany jerked back.

Jonah blinked, dazed, lips parted, trying to read her expression in the dim blue shadows of the tent.

Was she scared?

Regretful?

Still wanting him?

He couldn't tell.

He was trying so hard to understand—

Then came the sound.

ZZZZZZIIIIIPPPPP.

The unmistakable flap of a tent zipper being torn open.

Both of them froze.

"Oh no," Brittany whispered.

"Oh yes," Jonah whispered back.

Janessa's silhouette was highlighted by the campfire and she lurched toward them in the dark.

Her foot caught the guyline.

There was a split second where she hovered in mid-air like a tragic, chaotic ballerina—

Then she screamed.

And *fell. directly. on top of them.*

The tent buckled instantly.

Canvas collapsed.

Poles snapped inward.

Snow puffed up around Janessa like somebody had detonated a glitter bomb of misery.

Jonah grunted.

Brittany yelped.

Janessa shrieked, "WHY DOES THIS ALWAYS HAPPEN TO ME?!"

The entire micro-tent crumpled into a pathetic fabric pancake with three humans tangled inside like overstuffed laundry.

Somewhere in the distance, Trevor yelled proudly, "JANESSA HAS BREACHED!"

The tent was no longer a tent.

It was a tent avalanche.

A polyester crime scene.

A nylon body bag for dignity.

Two bodies struggled under the crumpled fabric like a cryptid sighting and the third one flailed on top.

Somewhere in the darkness:

"Ow—whose elbow is that—Britt? Jonah? OH MY GOD IS THIS YOUR KNEE ON MY SPLEEN?!"

"Janessa, calm down—"

"DO NOT TELL ME TO CALM DOWN, JONAH, I AM TRAPPED IN EMOTIONAL AND LITERAL DEBRIS—"

"Could everyone—just—stop—moving—" Brittany gasped, because she currently had Jonah's thigh wedged dangerously between hers and Janessa's elbow in her side.

The tent pole finally snapped with a sad little *twang* and the whole thing sagged lower, pressing Jonah even closer into Brittany's side.

And oh.

Oh no.

He was VERY close.

Jonah froze.

"Uh," he whispered into Brittany's ear, "your knee is—um—"

"My WHAT is where??"

"Touching... places."

She squeaked and tried to shift.

Which shoved Jonah's torso directly against hers.

"OH MY GOD GET YOUR BIG OUTDOOR MAN-THIGHS OFF MY FACE," Janessa screamed, flailing, kicking Jonah in the ribs.

"Ow—Janessa—stop thrashing—"

"I AM NOT THRASHING I AM SURVIVING."

"Brittany," Jonah whispered urgently, "I need you to move—like—two inches to the left."

"I CAN'T MOVE, I AM A HUMAN PRETZEL."

Someone outside cleared their throat.

"Uh... you guys okay over there?" a PA called hesitantly.

All three voices answered in a horrifying harmony:

"NO."

Steph was cackling somewhere behind the monitors.

Finally, FINALLY, Jonah managed to push up enough fabric to create an escape hole.

Cold air rushed in.

He grabbed the edge of the sleeping bag and practically rolled Brittany out into the snow like a fragile, confused cinnamon bun.Then he crawled out behind her, cheeks flushed, body heaving.

Janessa was still thrashing like a dramatic Victorian ghost.

"WHY IS IT DARK—IS THIS THE END—TELL MY FOLLOWERS I LOVED THEM—"

Brittany and Jonah collapsed into the snowbank, panting, disoriented, STILL touching because they hadn't actually untangled fully.

Brittany blinked up at the sky, breath fogging.

"I think," she said weakly, "I just died."

Jonah huffed a laugh, lying beside her, his hand still half tangled in the hem of her thermal shirt.

"Yeah," he agreed, "but... you almost kissed me first."

She froze.

He froze.

Janessa shrieked, "ARE YOU TWO MAKING OUT WHILE I SUFFER?"

"Absolutely not," Jonah called back, voice cracking.

Brittany wasn't so sure.

Janessa, the Furious Snow Dragon

Janessa did not simply *untangle herself from* the collapsed tent.

No.

She erupted from it.

She surged in a tangle of limbs, hair, and fury, looking exactly like a snow dragon who'd been wronged by several kingdoms.

"WHO DID THIS TO ME?!" she screeched, flinging a handful of snow dramatically to the sky like she was summoning a blizzard.

Trevor peeked from his tent flap, half asleep.

"Trevor senses unrest."

Janessa pointed at him like a wrathful Greek goddess.

"YOU! YOU SNORE LIKE A MOTORBIKE ON FIRE!"

Trevor blinked slowly, confused and unbothered.

"Trevor apologizes for his powerful lung capacity."

Janessa let out a sound that was somewhere between a scream, a sob, and an angry goose.

Steph, watching from behind the camera crew, clapped once, sharply.

"Alright, enough." She strode forward like she was wrangling toddlers instead of fully-grown adults. "New sleeping arrangements!"

Everyone straightened, sensing drama.

Steph pointed at Jonah and Brittany, her smile wicked.

"You two — cabin seven."

Both froze as they were pulling on their snow gear.

Brittany's stomach plummeted.

Jonah's heart slammed into his ribs.

Steph added, far too casually:

"It has a queen bed, a heater, and four walls that won't collapse when certain people fall into them."

Jonah coughed.

Brittany's face flushed so hard it probably melted nearby snow.

"And me?" Janessa demanded.

"Oh," Steph said sweetly, "you get to rebuild the tent you destroyed."

Janessa blinked.

"The— broken one?"

"Yes. The mangled one."

"I have to— sleep in *that*??"

Steph patted her shoulder with chilly sympathy.

"Well, unless you want to go back to Trevor."

Trevor looked up, deeply wounded.

"Trevor wishes to comfort her in her time of exile."

Janessa screamed again.

She kicked the ruined tent and it collapsed even further, somehow achieving a new level of pathetic.

Steph gave Jonah and Brittany a little shooing motion.

"Cabin. Now. Before the universe gives me a heart attack."

Brittany opened her mouth to object — or panic — or faint —

But Jonah gently touched her elbow.

"Come on," he said quietly.

And she went with him.

Because what choice did she have with the entire film crew watching—and the ghost of a kiss still sitting warm on her lips?

Terms & Conditions of Survival (Not Optional)

The PA drove them on a skidoo to Cabin Seven like a cheerful executioner.

"Okay! Rules!" she chirped, swinging the door open. "No outside gear because we need realism. Thermals only. Blanket stays on the bed. Cameras will pick up audio only unless we say otherwise. And remember—" she wiggled her eyebrows, "—sharing body heat is highly encouraged."

Brittany stared.

Jonah stared harder.

The cabin was... also tiny.

Like, **junior-sized shoebox** tiny.

One queen bed — a queen by *technicality*, by legal definition only, the kind that hotels call a queen but actually feels like two twin mattresses whispering secrets.

One small heater humming valiantly in the corner.

One window, frosted over.

And one blanket on the bed — just thick enough, just warm enough... if two people slept pressed together like a pair of cuddling otters.

Brittany inhaled sharply.

"Oh, hell no," she said.

The PA smiled sweetly. "Oh, hell yes. Goodnight!"

The door slammed behind her.

Silence.

Crackling heater.

Two heartbeats.

Brittany scowled at the bed like it had personally wronged her.

Jonah rubbed the back of his neck, trying desperately not to look like he wanted to fling himself onto it with her.

"Thermals?" he asked, clearing his throat.

She glared.

He lifted his hands in surrender. "Just making sure we're following the rules."

Brittany spun away, unzipping her jacket with militaristic efficiency. "Turn around."

Jonah nodded, turned, and shed his coat with a deep exhale, like stripping down to form-fitting thermals wasn't about to ruin him emotionally.

The thermals hugged every inch of him — broad shoulders, trim waist, long legs. He looked like a sculpture some Nordic god chiseled for fun.

Brittany caught his reflection in the frosted window.

And nearly died. It had been too dark in the tent to see what they looked like stripped down.

Her own thermals weren't helping. They covered everything... but softened nothing. They outlined curves she'd tried to ignore for years, highlighted the lines of her hips, the dip of her waist, the tension bunching in her shoulders.

Jonah turned around.

Stopped.

Went still.

Completely, utterly still.

His throat bobbed.

"Britt," he said softly.

She tried to fire sarcasm. Tried desperately.

Nothing came out.

He stepped forward carefully — like approaching a wild animal he didn't want to startle.

"Blanket?" he offered.

Her voice was thin. "Sure."

They approached the bed at the same time.

And realized simultaneously that:

A) There was no way to avoid touching.

B) The heater was not enough.

C) The blanket would only work if they lay close.

D) They were already breathing harder.

Jonah blew out a slow breath. "Okay. Ground rules."

Brittany crossed her arms. "Why do you get to make the rules?"

"I don't," he said gently. "We can make them together."

Damn him.

Damn him and his emotional maturity.

"Fine," she muttered. "Rule one: no talking about feelings."

Jonah's mouth twitched. "Rule one: amended — we can talk about feelings if one of us is literally dying."

"Rule one: no talking unless absolutely necessary," she tried again.

"Deal," he said. "Rule two: we share the blanket. No arguing."

Her jaw clenched. "Fine."

"Rule three," he murmured, voice dipping — dangerous, steady, deliberate — "if I... accidentally touch you in my sleep, you don't kick me off the bed."

She stared at him. Hard.

"Rule four," she countered, "if *I* accidentally touch *you*—you don't make a thing of it."

His eyes warmed. Just slightly.

"Never," he whispered.

A beat.

They climbed into bed.

Facing each other first.

Big mistake.

Huge.

Because their knees brushed. Their hands collided. Their breaths tangled.

"Turn around," Brittany blurted.

"Yeah," Jonah whispered, swallowing. "Good idea."

They turned.

She faced the wall. He faced her back.

The blanket slipped over both of them… perfectly… if they lay flush together.

So Jonah inched closer.

And closer.

Until his chest touched her spine.

Until his arm slid carefully — carefully — around her waist.

Until his legs curved behind hers.

She froze.

Then breathed.

Then melted. Just a fraction. Just enough for him to feel it.

Jonah's voice came low, almost pained:

"Is this okay?"

She nodded.

He exhaled shakily into her hair.

Minutes passed.

Warm. Quiet. Too intimate.

Then—

"Why did you run today?" Jonah asked softly.

She stiffened. "Rule one."

"Britt."

She closed her eyes tight.

He pressed his forehead between her shoulder blades, breath warm through the thin fabric.

Her pulse thundered.

"I thought *I* was going to kiss you," he added, voice breaking slightly. "And it scared me. But not in the way you think."

"Jonah…"

"No. Listen."

His arm tightened around her, just a little.

"When you left nine years ago, everything went grey. And now—" his voice caught, "—seeing you again… everything came back at once."

Brittany swallowed. Hard.

He kept going, quiet and wrecked.

"And when you walked away again today? It felt the same. I can't pretend it didn't."

Tears prickled her eyes.

"I didn't walk away because I wanted to," she whispered.

Jonah stilled behind her.

She breathed out: fragile, trembling.

"I walked away because if I stayed... I would've kissed you. Again. And I can't afford to want things I can't keep."

The words broke between them.

Slowly... painfully... Jonah shifted, turning her gently so she lay facing him.

Their noses nearly touched.

Their legs tangled under the blanket.

He cupped the back of her neck, thumb brushing her jaw.

"You don't know what you can keep," he whispered. "Not yet."

Her breath trembled.

She didn't kiss him.

He didn't kiss her.

But the space between them burned.

She finally whispered:

"Jonah... I'm scared."

He slid his forehead against hers.

"Me too," he murmured. "But I'm here."

She closed her eyes.

And for the first time in nine years—

She let him hold her.

Cabin Seven

The heater clicked softly in the corner, blowing just enough warm air to keep the room habitable. Brittany lay tucked against Jonah's chest, rigid as an icicle pretending it wasn't melting.

Jonah's hand moved slowly—carefully—up her arm, fingertips brushing the curve of her shoulder through the thin thermal fabric. Not possessive. Not demanding.

Just... there.

"Britt," he murmured, voice warm against the back of her neck. "You know the whole point of this show is to fall in love, right?"

She didn't turn. Didn't breathe. But he felt the tiny tug at the edge of her mouth anyway.

She smirked.

"No," she said quietly, almost smug, "the point is to win."

Jonah let out a soft laugh—low, deep, the kind that vibrated against her spine.

"You know we can do both," he said. "It's a couple that wins. Not just one person."

The word *couple* dropped like a stone in the small cabin.

He felt her body stiffen instantly, every muscle drawing tight under his arm.

"Britt—"

"I've already been derailed for nine years, Jo," she whispered, voice cracking in a way she couldn't hide. "I'm already so far behind."

He froze.

Not because she pulled away—she didn't. Not because she broke down—she didn't. But because of the quiet, hollow shame in her voice.

That was the part that gutted him.

Jonah closed his eyes.

Their noses brushed. Their legs tangled. Their breaths mingled in the inches between them.

He touched his forehead gently to hers.

"Hey," he whispered. "Look at me."

She didn't.

But she didn't run, either.

"You're not behind," he said, voice low and steady, like he could anchor her with the sound alone. "You're not derailed. You are exactly where you're supposed to be."

Her throat worked around a tight swallow.

"Lying in a cabin in the Arctic? On a ridiculous show? In thermals?"

He smiled, barely there.

"With me," he corrected softly.

Brittany's breath paused—quiet, involuntary.

He cupped the side of her face, thumb brushing the edge of her cheekbone, tender in a way she wasn't prepared for.

A tear slipped from the corner of her eye.

She tried to turn her face away.

Jonah caught it gently with his thumb.

"You're not behind," he repeated, almost a vow. "You're just... finally catching up to your own story."

Her mouth trembled.

She whispered, raw and defenceless:

"Jonah..."

And he didn't kiss her.

God, he wanted to.

But instead, he pressed his forehead into hers, breathing her in, holding her together piece by piece in the dark of Cabin Seven.

Blanket Theft & Thermals of Chaos

Brittany would've placed money—actual money, not just pride—that she wouldn't fall asleep. Not in a tiny cabin. Not in a too-small bed. Not wrapped in Jonah's warmth like a human burrito she definitely wasn't emotionally ready for.

But she lost that bet.

Hard.

Because she woke up freezing.

Frozen-solid Disney princess cold.

She blinked into the dark room, breath puffing little white clouds.

And then she realized—

The blanket was gone.

Stolen.

And Jonah... Jonah was wrapped in it like a smug cinnamon roll.

"Jo," she hissed into the darkness.

No response.

Great.

She shivered harder, curling in on herself, hands numb, nose actually painful from the cold. The heater was doing its best but without the blanket?

She was a Freezee.

"Jonah," she tried again, sharper.

Still nothing.

He was dead asleep, breathing slow and deep, body relaxed in the one toasty spot in the entire Canadian North.

Her teeth chattered.

Fine.

Fine.

If he wasn't going to wake up, she was going to survive this her own way.

She scooted closer.

Then she just went for it—slipping her icy hands under the hem of his thermal shirt and pressing her frozen nose directly into the warm curve of his neck.

The reaction was immediate.

Jonah **launched** out of the bed like he'd been tasered.

"JESUS—Britt!" he gasped, staggering backward, hands flying everywhere like he was fighting off a ghost.

Brittany sat bolt upright, hair a full disaster, still shaking.

"Well maybe if you didn't STEAL THE BLANKET like some giant, unconscious raccoon, I wouldn't be freezing to DEATH!"

Jonah blinked at her, dazed, shirt rumpled, hair sticking up in soft tufts.

"I didn't— I wasn't— why were your hands *under my shirt*?!"

"Because they were cold, Jonah!" she snapped, offended by his offense. "You were the only heat source available!"

He stared at her.

She glared back.

And then—

He snorted.

Actually snorted.

"You shoved your icicle fingers into my ribs."

"You hogged the entire blanket!"

"It was an accident!"

"MY DEATH WOULD HAVE BEEN AN ACCIDENT."

Jonah scrubbed a hand over his face, still half-asleep, still breathing too fast, still looking at her like she was ridiculous and going to be the end of him.

"Get back in the bed," he muttered, grabbing the blanket and flinging half of it toward her.

"No," she grumbled, still indignant. "You'll just steal it again."

"I won't."

"You will."

"I'll hold onto you this time," he said, way too casually for the 3 A.M. tension crackling between them.

She froze.

He froze.

The air thickened.

Then, softer:

"Come here, Britt," he murmured, not quite a plea, not quite a command.

And damn it all...

She went.

Brittany hesitated at the edge of the mattress, the blanket clutched around her shoulders like a defensive cloak.

Jonah stood there, thermal shirt riding up one side where she'd shoved her hands. He looked wrecked. He looked warm. He looked... inviting.

"Come here," he murmured again, voice still sandpaper-soft with sleep as he crawled back onto the bed.

Her stomach did the thing. The thing she pretended didn't happen. The thing that felt like falling and flying at the same time.

"Fine," she muttered, even though it was *not* fine and definitely not neutral.

Still— She crawled back into the bed.

Jonah followed, settling the blanket and sliding in behind her. But this time?

Oh, this time he didn't wait for the universe to dictate positions.

He wrapped an arm around her waist. Pulled her gently against him. Settled his chin in the curve of her neck. Pressed one warm, steadying hand low on her stomach, fingers spreading like he meant to anchor her in place.

Brittany forgot how lungs worked.

"You're still cold," he murmured, voice muffled against her skin.

He tugged her closer — impossibly closer — their legs slotting together like some cosmic puzzle finally aligned.

"You don't have to freeze alone, Britt," Jonah murmured. "Not anymore."

She melted.

Like marshmallow in hot cocoa. Like a glacier regretting all its life choices.

She didn't say thank you. She didn't say anything. But slowly, quietly, she reached down and laced their fingers together under the blanket.

Jonah's breath caught.

And this time?

Neither of them fell asleep pretending not to touch.

Morning Chaos — Featuring Trevor the Menace

Brittany woke up slowly, warm all over, wrapped in something that felt suspiciously like—

A human furnace.

Jonah's arm.

No, Jonah's *arms.*

Plural.

He had one under her head, one around her waist, one leg tangled with hers, and his face buried in her hair like he'd decided this was his new default sleeping position.

Warm breath brushed her shoulder.

Her entire body hummed.

She didn't dare move.

And then—

KNOCK KNOCK KNOCKKNOCKKNOCKKNOCKKNOCK—

Brittany jolted so hard she headbutted Jonah's chin.

Jonah groaned loudly.

Trevor's voice boomed through the door with the enthusiasm of seven golden retrievers stacked inside a trench coat.

"HELLO ROOM SERVICE! TREVOR SENSES CANOODLING!"

Brittany choked on air.

Jonah slapped a hand over his face.

Trevor knocked again, louder.

"TREVOR HAS COFFEE BUT ONLY IF YOU OPEN THE DOOR LOOKING DISHEVELED AND GUILTY."

"Go away," Jonah groaned, voice hoarse enough to start wars.

"TREVOR WILL NOT," Trevor replied cheerfully. "TREVOR SMELLS ROMANCE."

"Trevor," Brittany snapped, "you literally can't smell anything, it's thirty below—"

Trevor gasped dramatically. "SO YOU *ARE* TOGETHER IN THE BED. TREVOR KNEW."

Jonah half-crawled, half-rolled out of the covers and stomped toward the door in his thermals like a man preparing to fistfight destiny.

"DO NOT OPEN THAT DOOR," Brittany whisper-screeched. "YOUR THERMALS ARE SHOWING EVERYTHING."

Jonah looked down.

He was, in fact, very much on display.

Trevor banged again.

Jonah groaned louder and reached for his pants.

Brittany buried her head under the blanket.

This was their life now.

The competition announcement came with coffee and false optimism.

Everyone gathered outside again, bundled up, blinking into the pale morning light. The snow glittered deceptively, crisp and powdery, the kind that looked festive and absolutely refused to cooperate with human plans.

Steph stood beside a folding table that held a single laminated card and a whistle she absolutely did not need.

"Good morning," she sang. "Hope you're feeling creative."

That was never good.

"Today's challenge," Steph continued, "is simple."

She paused, smiling like someone who enjoyed the word *simple* far too much.

"You'll be building the biggest snowman."

There was a beat.

Then Wade frowned. "With... this snow?"

He scooped up a handful and watched it spill through his fingers like sugar.

Steph nodded. "Yes."

Aaliyah squinted at the ground. "It doesn't pack."

"Correct," Steph said cheerfully. "It is the wrong kind of snow."

Brittany laughed under her breath. Jonah huffed.

Trevor raised a hand. "Is this a metaphor?"

"No," Steph replied. "This is television."

She clapped once. "You'll have forty minutes. Use whatever you can find. Snow, ice, branches, ingenuity, desperation. Biggest wins. Wade and Aaliyah—"

She pointed at them.

"—you have immunity for keeping your tent intact and, quote, 'making the most of the situation.' You're still allowed to build for pride, but you cannot be eliminated."

Wade nodded solemnly. "We will honour the snow."

Aaliyah grinned. "We will not."

Steph turned to the rest. "Everyone else? Compete."

The whistle blew.

Chaos followed.

Jonah and Brittany stared at the snow for a long moment.

"This isn't happening," Brittany said.

Jonah crouched, tried packing a handful anyway. It immediately collapsed. "We're going to have to cheat."

She smiled. "Creatively."

They started scraping snow into shallow piles, layering it over chunks of ice Jonah pried loose with a shovel. It was slow, awkward, and deeply unglamorous, but something vaguely snowman-shaped began to emerge.

Nearby, Trevor and Janessa approached the problem like engineers.

Janessa squinted at the terrain. "We need a base that doesn't hate us."

Trevor nodded. "Ice core."

They dragged over a frozen chunk the size of a cooler and began sculpting around it, using snow more as decoration than structure. It wasn't tall yet, but it was solid.

Meanwhile...

Josh sat on a snowbank, sipping coffee.

Kelsey leaned against him, arms crossed, watching the others work.

"So," she said. "Are we...?"

Josh glanced at the snow, then at the frantic effort unfolding around them. "I don't think the universe wants us to win a snowman competition."

Kelsey smiled faintly. "Same."

They half-heartedly rolled a small ball of snow that immediately disintegrated.

Josh shrugged. "We tried."

"Did we?" she asked.

"Emotionally."

They abandoned it entirely and wandered closer to the cameras, hands in pockets, chatting about what they'd order first once they were home.

Time passed.

Steph prowled between teams, commentary relentless.

"Ooo, innovation!"

"Is that structural integrity or blind hope?"

"Josh and Kelsey... bold choice doing nothing."

Steph nodded. "It's saying a lot."

When the whistle blew again, everyone stepped back to assess.

Jonah and Brittany's snowman leaned precariously but stood, lumpy and earnest. Trevor and Janessa's creation was taller, sleeker, held together by stubbornness and physics.

Josh and Kelsey's snowman was... symbolic.

Steph walked the line, clipboard in hand.

After a moment, she turned.

"Well," she said. "This was enlightening."

Steph faced Josh and Kelsey.

"You two," she said gently, "did not build the biggest snowman."

Josh nodded. "No."

"Nor did you build a medium snowman."

"Correct."

"Nor," Steph continued, "did you appear particularly invested."

Kelsey shrugged. "We're very invested in not freezing."

Steph smiled, almost fond. "Honestly? Respect."

She took a breath.

"Josh and Kelsey, your journey ends here."

There was no gasp. No outrage.

They said their goodbyes easily, warmly. Kelsey hugged Brittany tight. Josh clapped Jonah on the shoulder.

"Good luck," he said. "You two feel... real."

Brittany swallowed and smiled. "Thank you."

Steph clapped her hands again.

"All right," she announced brightly. "Who's ready to go inside and process their feelings with carbs?"

Everyone groaned.

Steph grinned.

"Excellent."

Steph's Next Challenge — Operation Jealousy Arc

Breakfast had barely wrapped, when Steph strutted into the dining hall like a woman about to announce the royal games.

Clipboard hugged to her chest. Eyes sparkling with malicious producer delight. Ponytail swishing with violent purpose.

"GOOD MORNING, MY STAR-CROSSED SUGAR CUBES!"

Every contestant froze mid-bite.

Even Trevor stopped flexing.

Jonah and Brittany exchanged a look — wary, resigned, and a little traumatized. Steph never sounded this gleeful unless someone was about to cry on camera or accidentally confess something heart-breaking.

She clapped sharply.

"Time for your NEXT CHALLENGE!"

The group groaned.

Steph ignored them and continued, eyes laser-focused on Jonah and Brittany in a way that made Brittany's skin crawl.

"This challenge," Steph announced, pacing dramatically, "is about EMOTIONAL INTIMACY. CHEMISTRY."

Trevor raised his hand. "Trevor is ready."

Steph waved him off like a fruit fly.

"But FIRST," she said, voice rising with dangerous excitement, "we will be forming NEW PAIRS!"

Jonah stiffened.

Brittany stiffened harder.

Steph smiled like a Bond villain.

"Jonah... you're with Aaliyah."

Aaliyah gasped, flipping her hair like she'd been waiting for this moment her entire life. Jonah blinked. Hard. He gave Brittany a tiny flick of panic in his eyes.

Brittany's stomach dropped. Not a lot. Just enough to make her want to vomit into her mimosa.

"And Brittany," Steph continued sweetly, "you're with—"

She paused.

Let the silence simmer.

Let the tension tighten.

Let the cameras zoom in.

"Trevor."

Trevor fist-pumped so hard his chair tipped over.

"TREVOR ACCEPTS HIS DESTINY."

Brittany went pale.

Jonah went... blank. Composed. Totally neutral.

Which was the exact expression of a man who was being eaten alive on the inside.

Steph nearly sang as she stepped back.

"All right! Jonah and Aaliyah will complete the **Ice Carving Trust Task**, while Brittany and Trevor will handle the **Couples Winter Photoshoot Extravaganza.** The other couples, you will be doing trust falls outside so dress warm kids."

"Oh no," Jonah said quietly.

"Oh NO," Brittany said louder.

Trevor clapped like a toddler at Christmas.

"Aaliyah," Steph continued, "you and Jonah will carve a seven-foot ice sculpture representing the theme of 'Shared Vision.'"

Aaliyah wriggled her eyebrows at Jonah like she was already posing on their future wedding website.

"And Brittany," Steph added, "you will be modelling in a cozy couple's photoshoot with Trevor."

Trevor beamed. "Trevor has very photogenic pectorals."

Brittany nearly blacked out from second-hand embarrassment.

Then Steph lowered her voice into a giddy whisper.

"And don't worry, viewers love jealousy arcs. They EAT this stuff."

Jonah and Brittany locked eyes across the room.

Neither said a word.

But the firestorm brewing between them was unmistakable:

Don't fall for Aaliyah. Don't let Trevor touch you.

The games had officially begun.

Trevor & Brittany

The production crew had set up two "challenge zones" in the clearing—one for Jonah and Aaliyah's ice-carving task, and one for Brittany and Trevor's couple's photoshoot.

They were close.

Too close.

Close enough that anything happening in one zone could be seen—loudly, dramatically—from the other.

Because Steph had personally moved the equipment *"three feet to the left"* with the kind of malicious precision usually reserved for DC supervillains.

"Perfect!" Steph clapped, surveying the barely-separated spaces. "Close enough for... inspiration."

Paige whispered, "You mean jealousy." Steph whispered back, "Synonyms."

They were sent away to change and Brittany had a choice of a ski bunny bikini or a one-piece bathing suit that somehow left less to the imagination. She chose the bikini.

Brittany stood in front of the photo setup—a rustic wooden bench, a fake log fire, a plaid blanket draped like a romance novel cover, and a collection of props that screamed *Pinterest threw up.*

Trevor struck a pose beside her, he was dressed in a boy-short swimsuit , arms crossed, pectorals flexed at the Northern Lights in gratitude.

"TREVOR IS READY FOR PASSIONATE IMAGERY," he declared.

Brittany pinched the bridge of her nose. "I can't believe this is my life."

The photographer—a skinny guy with a beanie and artistic despair in his eyes—lifted his camera.

"Okay! Brittany, scoot closer to Trevor. Pretend you're a loving couple."

Brittany moved **one inch** closer.

The photographer groaned. "No, like you actually LIKE him."

Trevor grinned. "Trevor is extremely lovable."

Brittany muttered, "Debatable."

Meanwhile, Jonah and Aaliyah were directly in her peripheral vision. Aaliyah giggled. Jonah handed her a carving tool. Their heads bent close like they were sculpting the ninth wonder of the world.

"Trevor senses tension in the air," he whispered theatrically. "Trevor breathes it in deeply."

"Stop breathing it in," she snapped.

The photographer waved. "Okay, pose time! Trevor, sit behind Brittany and wrap your arms around her like you're keeping her warm."

Brittany's soul briefly left her body.

"No," she said immediately.

"YES," Steph said from somewhere behind a birch tree.

"Brittany," Trevor murmured dramatically, "Trevor vows to keep you warm with his radiant body heat."

"I'd rather freeze."

Trevor wrapped his arms around her anyway—too close, too enthusiastic, way too flexible.

"Trevor feels spiritual energy," he whispered.

"I feel harassment," she muttered.

The photographer snapped photos like a man being paid in adrenaline shots.

Then—

Aaliyah giggled again.

Loudly.

Brittany's head whipped in that direction.

Jonah was laughing softly at something Aaliyah said, breath fogging in the cold air, his face warm and open.

He never looked like that with the other women here.

With Brittany, yes—once, years ago. With anyone else? Never.

Until now.

Her stomach plunged.

Trevor leaned forward into the moment like the world's worst cupid.

"Trevor recommends jealous eye contact," he whispered helpfully. "Make him feel it."

"I'm not jealous."

"You are staring like you want to melt her with your mind."

Brittany snapped away from the view like she'd been caught spying.

"I'm not jealous!" she insisted.

Trevor raised an eyebrow. "Trevor is highly educated in emotional subtext."

The photographer groaned again.

"Brittany, honey, can you soften your expression? You look... furious."

"I *am* furious."

"Great! Use it."

Jonah looked up right then—from across the clearing—and saw Trevor wrapped around her from behind, his chin nearly on her shoulder, their bodies practically tangled.

Jonah's expression went still.

The ice-sculpting chisel slipped.

Aaliyah gasped, "Careful!"

Jonah didn't even answer.

He was too busy staring at Brittany like he'd just been stabbed in the soul.

Brittany blinked.

A slow, careful warmth trickled through her chest.

"Trevor..." she murmured.

"Trevor hears your heart accelerating."

"Let go of me."

Trevor nodded solemnly. "Trevor respects emotional journey."

And he dropped his arms immediately.

Across the clearing, Jonah visibly exhaled.

Brittany didn't know what that meant.

But she felt it anyway.

Jonah & Aaliyah – The Ice Carving Meltdown

The ice block stood taller than Jonah, gleaming under the morning light like a frozen monolith of doom.

Aaliyah clasped her hands in excitement.

"Oh my God, Jonah! We get to carve something! This is gonna be so cute!"

It started off fun, they worked together well and had a few laughs even. Then...

"You okay?"

"Perfect," Jonah lied, the chisel shaking in his hand like he was trying to perform heart surgery in a snowstorm.

Aaliyah followed his line of sight.

Across the clearing.

Where Trevor had Brittany in a couples pose so aggressively romantic it bordered on red alert-level intrusion of personal space.

Trevor leaned in for the camera, whispering god-knows-what nonsense into Brittany's ear.

Brittany forced a smile that looked like she wanted to commit homicide.

Steph watched from behind a birch tree with the intensity of a wildlife photographer stalking a rare mating ritual.

Jonah's jaw flexed so hard the ice block might've felt it.

Aaliyah coughed delicately.

"Do you... need a moment?"

"No," Jonah snapped. A beat. "I'm fine."

He lifted the chisel.

And immediately carved a long, violent gouge straight through the center of the ice.

Aaliyah yelped. "HEY! That was going to be the heart shape!"

Jonah winced. "Sorry. My hand slipped."

Aaliyah stared at him.

"Your whole ARM slipped."

Jonah scrubbed his palm over his face.

Every time Trevor touched Brittany? He flinched.

Every time Brittany shifted away? He exhaled like he'd been underwater too long.

Aaliyah pressed her lips together, suppressing a knowing smile.

"Jonah."

He didn't look at her.

"Jonah."

Nothing.

"JONAH."

He jolted. "What?!"

She set the chisel down and tapped her manicured finger against his chest.

"So. You and Brittany."

He froze.

Harder than the ice block between them.

"There is no—Britt and I—nothing—nothing is—" Jonah waved vaguely at the world. "This is all... production manipulation."

Aaliyah smirked.

"Mm-hm. Then why are you shaking?"

"I'm COLD."

"You're wearing three layers."

Aaliyah leaned in conspiratorially.

"For the record?" she whispered. "I'm not trying to steal you."

Jonah blinked. "What?"

Aaliyah pointed her chin toward Brittany.

"Because I'd rather not get murdered by a girl staring at me like I stole her puppy and pushed it into a river."

Jonah followed her gaze.

Brittany was watching them.

Hard.

Trying not to look like she was watching them. Failing spectacularly.

When their eyes met across the clearing?

Brittany's expression flickered.

Jealousy. Fear. Want. Panic. Hope. Everything she didn't want to feel in front of cameras.

Aaliyah elbowed him gently.

"You're allowed to like her, you know."

Jonah didn't answer.

His eyes were locked on Brittany like they'd forgotten how to look anywhere else.

"Also?" Aaliyah added, shrugging casually. "She's into you."

Aaliyah laughed, patting his back as he coughed like a dying snowman.

"Oh my God, calm down!" she wheezed. "I didn't say propose to her—just admit that watching Trevor wrap himself around her is making you spiral."

Jonah glared.

Aaliyah only smirked wider.

"You can fake it with Steph. You can fake it with the cameras. But you cannot fake it with me."

He swallowed. Hard.

Aaliyah leaned closer, lowering her voice.

"Question," she whispered. "Do you want Brittany to be your partner?"

Jonah's throat bobbed.

He didn't LOOK AWAY.

Aaliyah nodded slowly.

"That's what I thought."

She handed him the chisel again.

"Now carve your feelings into this ice block before you explode."

Back to Brittany and Trevor

The photographer scrolled through the shots on his camera, brow furrowed, lips pursed in artistic distress. Then he glanced up and crooked a finger at Steph.

"Hey. Can I get a producer eye on these?"

Steph crossed the clearing, boots crunching softly in the snow, clipboard tucked under her arm. Brittany and Trevor were still posed near the bench, Trevor lounging like a man who believed gravity was optional, Brittany perched stiffly beside him, jaw tight, eyes flicking anywhere but Jonah.

Steph leaned over the camera.

Scrolled.

Paused.

Scrolled again.

She sighed.

Not loudly. Not dramatically.

But *deliberately.*

"I thought you were a model, Britt," she said, disappointment threaded just thick enough to sting. "These aren't selling the relationship."

Brittany's spine went rigid.

Trevor blinked. "Trevor feels personally attacked."

Steph didn't look at him.

She lifted her voice a fraction, just enough.

"Let's do it again, folks."

Jonah's chisel slipped from his hand and hit the ice with a sharp crack.

Steph saw it from the corner of her eye.

She hid her smile.

"This time," Steph continued breezily, turning back to the set, "let's sex it up a little, huh?"

Brittany's head snapped up.

"I want Trevor lying on the bench," Steph said, already rearranging the narrative in her head. "And Brittany... you're straddling him."

Jonah turned fully now.

Steph kept going.

"You can hover if you want," she added magnanimously, "but I want sex. I want feelings. I want everyone watching to *believe* you two have it bad for each other."

She clapped once.

"Let's go."

The clearing went still.

Trevor's grin faltered for the first time. Brittany's face went cold.

And Jonah—

Jonah vibrated.

Something sharp and righteous winding tight in his chest.

"No."

The word cut through the air like a blade.

Every head turned.

Jonah stepped forward, hands clenched at his sides.

"No," he said again, louder now. "You can't treat people like they're just props."

Steph turned slowly, eyebrows lifting in mock surprise.

"Oh?"

"This isn't a toy," Jonah snapped, gesturing between Brittany and Trevor. "You don't get to humiliate people just for a shot."

He was shaking.

Not with fear.

With restraint.

Steph had to physically stop herself from bouncing on her toes.

This was *excellent* television.

Then Brittany moved.

She stepped forward sharply, anger blazing across her face — not flustered, not embarrassed, but furious.

"Jonah—" she snapped.

He turned to her instantly.

"I don't need a saviour," she said, voice cutting and controlled. "I signed up for this show. I know exactly what happens."

Her eyes burned.

"Back off."

The words landed hard.

Jonah froze.

Not because she was wrong.

Because she meant it.

The clearing held its breath.

Steph smiled softly, like a woman who had just struck narrative gold.

Jonah took a slow, deliberate breath.

The kind you take when you know if you don't step away, you're about to do something irreversible.

He looked at Aaliyah, jaw tight, eyes still flicking helplessly toward Brittany across the clearing.

"I'll be back," he said quietly.

Aaliyah studied him for a beat, then nodded once. Gentle. Knowing.

Jonah turned and walked away, boots crunching toward the sauna confessional, shoulders rigid like he was holding himself together by sheer force of will.

The second he disappeared from view, Brittany exhaled.

It came out shaky. Raw. Like she'd been holding it in since the moment Steph opened her mouth.

She closed her eyes briefly.

Then opened them.

"Okay," she said, voice steady despite the storm in her chest. "Let's do the second shoot."

She straightened her spine, rolled her shoulders back, lifted her chin.

Armour on.

Trevor blinked at her, then smiled slowly, something like admiration flickering across his face.

"Well," he said, impressed, "Trevor respects a woman who chooses violence."

She shot him a look. "Lie down."

Trevor obeyed instantly, stretching out on the bench like a man who understood when a moment was bigger than his ego.

Steph clapped once.

"Remember," she called brightly, "sexy is the theme."

Brittany turned her head just enough to meet Steph's eyes.

And delivered the single dirtiest look Steph had ever received in her entire producing career.

It was lethal. Promising retribution.

Steph nearly purred.

Delightful, she thought.

The camera clicked.

And then—

For the next ten minutes, the Arctic didn't stand a chance.

Brittany straddled the bench, hovering just above Trevor, heat and intention pouring off her in waves. She knew her angles. Knew the power of a slow look, a parted mouth, the way to let desire read as dangerous instead of desperate.

Trevor matched her beat for beat, playful but grounded, letting her lead without dulling the chemistry.

The photographer's breath hitched. The crew forgot to shiver. Even the wind seemed to pause.

Across the clearing, Steph glanced toward the ice sculpture.

Jonah was back.

But he wasn't carving.

Steph watched it happen in real time.

The jealousy. The crack. The regret.

The realization that he'd walked away... and maybe walked away too far.

His shoulders sagged just slightly.

Not dramatic.

Steph's smile faded.

She knew the line.

She always did.

This was as far as she could push it without breaking something that wouldn't mend on camera.

"Okay!" Steph called suddenly. "That's enough! We're done here."

The photographer lowered the camera, dazed. Trevor sat up, blinking. The spell shattered.

Brittany slid off the bench, pulse racing, eyes blazing. She didn't look at Jonah. Didn't look at Steph.

She stalked away into the snow, tugging on the parka someone handed her, fury and adrenaline carrying her forward like a tide.

Steph watched her go.

Then glanced once more at Jonah.

Yeah.

That was enough damage for one day.

Staying in the Game

The sauna door closed behind Jonah with a dull thud.

Heat wrapped around him instantly, thick and suffocating, steam curling along the cedar walls like it had been waiting for him. He stood there for a moment, hands braced on the door, head bowed, breathing hard.

Then he laughed.

Once.

Sharp. Bitter.

"Jesus," he muttered.

He scrubbed a hand through his hair and finally turned toward the camera, which was already blinking red in the corner. No producer voice. No prompt.

Just him.

Jonah sat down on the wooden bench, elbows on his knees, chest rising and falling like he'd just run a mile.

"I walked away," he said quietly. "Because if I didn't… I was going to do something I couldn't take back."

He swallowed.

The heat beaded on his skin, sweat tracing down his spine, but he barely seemed to notice.

"I've spent nine years telling myself I missed the *idea* of Brittany," he continued. "That it was nostalgia. First love syndrome. Whatever makes it easier to live without her."

He shook his head slowly.

"That was a lie."

His jaw flexed.

"Watching her out there just now?" He let out a breath through his nose. "That wasn't jealousy about Trevor. That was fear."

He leaned back, staring at the ceiling like it might offer absolution.

"I'm terrified that she's learned how to survive without me so well... she doesn't need me anymore."

His voice dropped.

"And I don't get to be angry about that."

A beat.

"But God help me, it still hurts."

He looked back at the camera now, eyes dark, unguarded.

"When Steph talks about 'sexing it up,' about using people like props?" He scoffed softly. "That's not what set me off."

He rubbed his chest once, slow and unconscious.

"It was the idea that Brittany might think that's all she's worth. That she has to *perform* desire to stay in the game."

His eyes burned.

"She's always been more than that."

Silence filled the sauna, broken only by the hiss of steam.

Jonah's shoulders sagged.

"I walked away because I respect her," he said. "And because I don't trust myself to watch her pretend she doesn't matter to me."

He exhaled, long and heavy.

"And the worst part?" he added quietly. "Is that when she told me to back off..."

His mouth twisted.

"She was right."

He closed his eyes.

"I don't want to save her," he said. "I just want to stand beside her."

The camera lingered.

Jonah finally looked straight into the lens, voice steady but wrecked.

"And if she never chooses me?" he said. "I'll live with that."

A pause.

"But I won't be the man who pressures her into choosing *anything*."

He leaned forward again, forearms braced on his thighs.

"God," he whispered. "I love her."

The steam swallowed the words.

Brittany wasn't sure if she was furious, scared, or completely confused.

It was probably all three, tangled together into a tight, buzzing knot that sat just under her ribs and refused to settle.

She stalked away from the clearing, boots crunching too hard into the snow, breath coming sharp and fast. Her hands were clenched so tightly her fingers ached, nails biting into her palms like she could anchor herself there if she tried hard enough.

Jo.

Of course it was Jo.

Because when she'd snapped at him—when she'd told him to back off, sharp and defensive and a little too loud—he'd actually done it.

He hadn't argued. He hadn't pushed. He hadn't looked wounded just to make her feel guilty.

He'd backed off.

Respectfully.

That fact landed like a punch to the chest.

Damn him.

Damn him for listening. Damn him for respecting her boundary even when it clearly cost him something. Damn him for diffusing her anger when she wanted so badly to stay mad.

Anger was easier. Anger was clean. Anger didn't ask her questions she didn't want to answer.

And Trevor—

God.

Trevor, with his ridiculous grin and unexpected restraint. Trevor, who'd dropped his arms immediately when she asked. Trevor, who'd stood there like a golden retriever in a snowstorm, somehow offering support without making it weird or possessive or loaded.

That was not helpful.

None of this was helpful.

She stomped harder, jaw tight, heart racing like she was being chased—even though no one was following her. The cameras were behind her. The moment was behind her. The entire ridiculous setup was behind her.

Then she stopped.

Just... stopped.

Right there in the snow.

The cold air hit her lungs and she sucked in a breath so deep it almost hurt. Her shoulders sagged a fraction as the adrenaline finally loosened its grip.

And suddenly—the absurdity of it all punched through.

The cameras. The Arctic. The fact that she'd just nearly lost her mind over a staged photoshoot with a man who called himself Trevor in the third person.

She let out a short, surprised huff.

Then another.

Her mouth twitched before she could stop it.

A smirk crept in, sharp and incredulous.

She shook her head, breath fogging in front of her face.

"Oh my God," she muttered under her breath.

The smirk turned into a grin.

The grin cracked into laughter.

Not hysterical. Not broken.

Just real.

She laughed out loud, shoulders shaking, the sound ripping free like something she'd been holding back for too long.

"Okay," she said to herself, pressing a gloved hand to her chest as she caught her breath. "Okay. My life isn't in danger."

She glanced back once—toward the clearing, toward the chaos, toward him.

"This is just a game," she continued quietly. "A ridiculous, overproduced, emotionally manipulative game."

Her smile softened. Her spine straightened.

"Remember, Brittany," she said, firmer now. Grounded. "This is an opportunity. Not a threat. Not a trap."

She exhaled.

"Not anything more than that."

The laughter faded, but the steadiness stayed.

And with her head held a little higher and her armor locked back into place, Brittany turned and walked on—ready to play.

Brittany's Back

Jonah pushed the sauna door open and stepped out into the cold, the sharp Arctic air biting at his damp skin like it meant to wake him up.

Steam curled off his shoulders as he exhaled, head still buzzing from everything he'd said out loud in that cedar box. The confession. The truth. The ache he'd finally let breathe.

He was halfway through pulling his shirt back on when he heard it.

Laughter.

He froze.

Not the loud, performative kind that usually echoed through the lodge. Not the clipped, polite sound people made when they knew a camera was pointed at them.

This was different.

It was lighter. Warmer. Unguarded.

His head snapped up.

Across the clearing, a little distance away from the chaos, Brittany stood alone in the snow, her breath fogging in front of her face. Her shoulders shook. Her head tipped back just slightly. One hand pressed to her chest like she was surprised by the sound herself.

Jonah forgot to breathe.

Because that laugh—

That was her.

Not Brittany-the-contestant. Not Brittany-the-strategist. Not Brittany with her armour strapped on so tight it cut into her ribs.

That was the laugh she used to make when they were younger. When she'd lose an argument and accept it with humour instead of deflection. When something absurd caught her off guard and she let herself feel it.

The tightness in his chest loosened all at once, like a knot finally giving way.

He hadn't realized how badly he'd been braced for her anger. How convinced he'd been that he'd pushed too far, crossed a line, ruined something fragile before it even had the chance to exist again.

But she wasn't angry.

She wasn't breaking.

She was laughing.

A slow smile spread across his face before he could stop it. Small. Soft. Private.

Maybe things weren't completely ruined.

Maybe she was okay.

And maybe—just maybe—the door he'd been so careful not to push closed wasn't shut at all.

He watched her for another heartbeat, then turned away quietly, giving her the space she'd asked for... carrying that sound with him like a promise he wasn't ready to name.

Brittany decided, with sudden and startling clarity, that Janessa had earned the villain spot.

Not the misunderstood antagonist. Not the spicy rival. The full, dramatic, scenery-chewing villain.

And Brittany was not going to compete for it.

Every interaction with Janessa had the same result: Janessa spiraled. Louder. Bigger. More outrageous. Each comment landed like gasoline on a fire Brittany didn't have the emotional bandwidth to tend.

It wasn't that Brittany couldn't escalate.

She just didn't want to.

She didn't have it in her to scream, or posture, or be insecure for the cameras. Not when Janessa was already doing it with the enthusiasm of a woman auditioning for a daytime Emmy.

So Brittany made a decision.

If Janessa wanted to be the villain, Brittany would be... amused.

She let her posture loosen. Let the tension slip out of her shoulders. Let her expression settle into something just this side of smug. Not cruel. Not mean.

Just quietly superior.

The *I know something you don't* archetype.

The *I've read the script and I'm not panicking* energy.

And honestly?

It felt incredible.

She watched Janessa flail from a comfortable emotional distance, sipping her coffee like this was prestige television and not her real life. Every overreaction only made Brittany's calm feel sharper, more intentional.

Oh, you're spiraling? That's adorable.

The Elimination

The announcement came after lunch, which felt deliberate.

Steph gathered them in the kitchen, where the counters gleamed and the appliances sat there like temptations specifically designed to hurt feelings.

"Okay," she said brightly, clasping her hands. "Today's challenge is about creativity, adaptability, and not poisoning anyone."

Aaliyah narrowed her eyes. "I don't like the way you said that."

Steph smiled. "You're going to love the rest."

She gestured around the room. "You have one hour to cook something edible and attractive."

There was a collective exhale.

"And," Steph continued, "you may not use the oven. Or the stove. Or anything that produces heat."

Silence.

Jonah stared at the stovetop. "So... no cooking."

"Incorrect," Steph said cheerfully. "Just no cooking *as you know it.*"

Trevor raised a hand. "Is this a metaphor again?"

"No," Steph replied. "This is a test of vibes."

She turned slightly. "Brittany and Trevor—you have immunity from the photoshoot earlier today. You're still allowed to participate, but you cannot be eliminated."

Brittany blinked. "I'm sorry, I have *what* with Trevor?"

Trevor grinned. "Don't worry. Trevor will be normal."

Jonah snorted.

Steph clapped. "Hour starts now."

The kitchen exploded into motion.

Jonah and Brittany exchanged a look.

"Cold plates?" Brittany suggested.

"Charcuterie-adjacent," Jonah said immediately. "But elevated."

They moved in sync without discussing it further, pulling out boards, arranging fruit, slicing cheese with quiet focus. Jonah layered textures. Brittany fussed with spacing like this was a gallery installation.

Nearby, Trevor and Janessa approached the task cautiously.

Janessa stared into the fridge. "We could do a salad."

Trevor nodded. "We could also do... a better salad."

They started assembling something thoughtful and balanced, chopping carefully, tasting as they went. It wasn't flashy, but it was composed.

Aaliyah and Wade stood frozen for a beat.

"No heat?" Wade asked.

"No heat," Aaliyah confirmed.

Wade opened the fridge, scanned its contents. "We're very good at warm food."

Aaliyah sighed. "We're emotionally a stew."

They rallied anyway, pulling out ingredients with determination. Wade mashed something aggressively. Aaliyah tried to shape it into something presentable.

Time ticked down.

Plates came together.

Jonah and Brittany's board looked effortless. Colourful. Intentional. It said *we planned this*, even though they hadn't.

Trevor and Janessa's dish was clean, simple, quietly appealing.

Aaliyah and Wade's... tried.

Wade stepped back, head tilted. "It's... rustic."

Aaliyah pinched the bridge of her nose. "It looks like it lost a fight."

Steph arrived like a shark sensing blood.

"All right," she said. "Let's taste."

She sampled each dish with exaggerated seriousness, scribbling notes, nodding thoughtfully.

Finally, she straightened.

"This was harder than it looked," Steph said. "Some of you understood the assignment."

Her gaze flicked to Brittany and Jonah. "Presentation."

Then to Trevor and Janessa. "Restraint."

Then to Aaliyah and Wade.

"And some of you," Steph continued gently, "are better at surviving storms than making raw food seductive."

Aaliyah laughed immediately. Wade groaned.

Steph took a breath.

"Aaliyah. Wade. Your journey ends here."

There was no shock. Just acceptance.

Wade wrapped an arm around Aaliyah. "Honestly? Fair."

She nodded. "We are not cold-food people."

They hugged everyone, warmth radiating even as they prepared to leave. Aaliyah squeezed Brittany's hands.

"You're braver than you think," she said quietly.

Brittany swallowed. "So are you."

As they walked away, Wade called back, "If anyone turns on the stove, we will haunt you."

Steph clapped again.

"Okay!" she said brightly. "Who's hungry again?"

Everyone laughed.

Their next challenge came fast enough to keep Brittany from enjoying her newfound inner peace for too long.

Ice fishing.

Whoever caught the largest fish won.

The rules were announced with far too much cheer for an activity that involved sitting on frozen water voluntarily.

The last two couples would be paired with an Indigenous guide.

And of course—*of course*—Jonah and Brittany were "randomly" assigned together.

Brittany didn't even bother hiding her snort.

Jonah caught her eye and lifted one brow, lips twitching like he was trying very hard not to smile.

Their guide introduced himself as Toklo—a young man with an unreadable expression, sharp eyes, and a delivery so dry it made the Arctic look humid by comparison.

He led them across the ice with easy confidence, boots sure, movements unhurried.

"This," Toklo announced, stopping abruptly, "is my super secret magic fishing spot."

Brittany blinked.

Jonah looked around. "So... you bring everyone here?"

Toklo shrugged. "Only the ones I like."

Brittany trusted him immediately.

They began setting up, drilling into the ice while Toklo moved with quiet efficiency. Brittany was just settling onto her stool when something caught her eye.

A rifle.

Leaning casually against Toklo's gear.

A very real, very large rifle.

Her spine stiffened.

She stared at it. Then at him. Then back at the rifle.

Toklo noticed her look and grinned, entirely unbothered.

"Oh," he said easily. "That's for polar bears."

Brittany's stomach dropped.

"I'm sorry," she said carefully. "For *what*."

Toklo shrugged again, cheerful as ever.

"In case they show up," he said. "They like this spot too."

Jonah went very still.

Brittany let out a slow breath.

"Okay," she said. "So we're ice fishing... with bears... and a gun... on a reality show."

Toklo nodded. "Yes."

She stared out at the endless white.

"Well," she muttered, "at least Janessa isn't here."

Jonah laughed—real, startled laughter—and something warm settled between them despite the cold.

If this was the universe's idea of balance, Brittany decided, she could live with it.

"Aren't polar bears endangered?" Jonah asked, suddenly very focused on the legal ramifications of everything happening within a ten-foot radius.

He glanced at the rifle. Then at Toklo. Then at the endless stretch of white ice beneath their feet.

Toklo didn't even look up from adjusting the line.

He shrugged, casual as a man discussing the weather. "They don't seem to know that," he said. "Not when they want to eat you."

Jonah's mouth opened.

Closed.

Opened again.

Brittany felt something cold and sharp crawl straight up her spine.

"Eat us?" she repeated, voice a half-octave higher than usual.

Technically, she knew this.

Of course she did.

She was Canadian. Polar bears were practically a national PSA. Every childhood came with some variation of: *don't run, don't provoke, and if you see one you're already in trouble.*

Still—knowing something academically and hearing a man say it while standing on frozen water with a gun nearby were two very different experiences.

Toklo finally looked at her, eyes bright with amusement.

"Yeah," he said, nodding once. "They like to hunt us back."

Brittany stared at him.

Jonah stared at him harder.

Toklo grinned.

"Fair's fair."

There was a long, fragile silence.

The wind whispered across the ice.

Somewhere far too close in Brittany's imagination, a polar bear considered its lunch options.

Jonah swallowed.

"So," he said carefully, "statistically speaking... how often does that happen?"

Toklo tilted his head, thinking. "Not often," he said. A beat. "But often enough to bring the rifle."

Brittany slowly reached out and placed her gloved hand on Jonah's sleeve, anchoring herself to something warm and alive and not apex-predator-shaped.

"Okay," she said briskly. "Great. Fantastic. Love that for us."

Jonah leaned closer to her, voice low. "If we survive this, I'm never complaining about traffic again."

She snorted despite herself.

Toklo crouched, peering down into the fishing hole like this was all perfectly normal.

"Relax," he added. "If a bear shows up, you'll know."

Brittany's eyes widened again. "How?"

Toklo glanced back at her, grin sharp and unapologetic.

"You'll feel very small," he said. "And very slow."

Jonah made a noise that might've been a prayer.

Brittany squeezed his arm.

"Okay," she muttered. "New rule. If a polar bear appears, I'm sacrificing Trevor first."

Jonah huffed a laugh, tension cracking just enough to breathe again.

Toklo chuckled softly. "Smart," he said. "He looked loud."

Fishing

Toklo moved with brisk efficiency, pulling supplies from his sled and setting up a wind break like he'd done this a thousand times before. Poles went in. Canvas snapped taut. The shelter rose quickly, angled just right to take the worst of the gusts.

The solo camera person took their position discreetly and quickly faded into the background.

When he was satisfied, he stepped back, hands on his hips, and turned his attention to the horizon.

Just... stared.

Jonah blinked.

"You're not going to show us how to do this?" he asked, holding up the fishing line like it might bite him.

Toklo glanced over his shoulder, unimpressed.

"You don't know how to fish?" he asked, the question carrying genuine disbelief and a rapidly thinning patience.

Jonah opened his mouth.

Brittany beat him to it.

"Oh my God," she said, rolling her eyes. "Jo—give me the line and the bait. I can set this up."

She shot Jonah a look, all fond exasperation and smug familiarity.

"Didn't you spend your summers on Ashby Lake with your grandfather?" she teased. "Or were you just floating around being decorative?"

Jonah huffed and handed her the gear. "I was swimming and tanning," he defended himself. "Not... this."

Toklo watched for half a second as Brittany threaded the line, checked the hook, and baited it with quick, practiced hands.

Satisfied, he turned back to the horizon.

Brittany noticed.

That tiny nod of approval landed like a gold star.

She crouched, motioning Jonah closer. "Okay. Watch. This part matters."

Jonah leaned in, their shoulders brushing as she guided his hands. Her voice dropped automatically, instinctively, like they'd done this kind of thing together a hundred times before.

"See how the line feeds here?" she said. "You don't want slack, but you don't want tension either. It's... balanced."

"Story of my life," Jonah muttered.

She smirked.

Then the wind picked up.

It didn't rush in all at once. It crept. A low moan sliding across the ice, building into a long, hollow howl that swept across the flat plain like it had nowhere else to go.

Brittany straightened slowly.

The sound wrapped around them, unbroken by trees or buildings or anything remotely human. Just snow. Ice. White stretching forever in every direction.

She shivered.

Some of it was the cold. The kind that worked its way through layers and settled deep in the bones.

And some of it was... something else.

This place was bleak.

Beautiful, yes—but stripped bare. No roads. No lights. No cabins tucked just out of sight.

No civilization.

Just them. And Toklo. And the rifle leaning casually against the sled.

Jonah glanced at her, brow furrowing. "You okay?"

She nodded, even as her fingers curled tighter around the line.

"Yeah," she said, honest but steady. "Just... forgot how big the world gets when there's nothing blocking it."

Toklo shifted his stance, eyes still scanning the horizon.

"It's loud today," he said calmly. "Storm might change its mind."

That did not help.

Brittany let out a slow breath and forced her shoulders to relax.

Okay, she told herself. You've got this.

Fishing line. Wind break. Jonah beside her.

She could handle bleak.

The Storm

They had just settled in.

Line set. Bait dropped. The wind howling low and constant, like it had opinions about their presence. Somewhere in the distance, the ice cracked—a deep, echoing sound that rolled across the flat white plain and settled in Brittany's chest.

She didn't like that sound.

Then Toklo went still.

Not tense. Not startled.

Still in the way of someone whose body knew something before his brain bothered to narrate it.

Brittany noticed immediately.

Jonah did too.

Toklo straightened slowly and turned, eyes narrowing as he scanned the horizon. His gaze locked onto a bank of dark clouds bruising the sky in the distance, moving faster than Brittany liked.

He nodded once to himself.

"Okay," he said calmly. "You've got about ten minutes to catch your fish."

Jonah blinked. "That's... encouraging?"

Toklo didn't smile.

"Then we're leaving," he continued. "Storm's heading this way. And it won't be a good one."

Brittany wasn't entirely sure what qualified as a *good* storm in the Arctic, but if this one didn't meet the criteria, she was very comfortable with the idea of not finding out.

She glanced at Jonah.

"Pack it in?" she asked, already reaching for the gear.

Jonah didn't hesitate. He nodded. "Pack it in."

They moved quickly and efficiently, dismantling the setup with a shared urgency that didn't require discussion. Line reeled in. Gear stacked. Canvas folded and strapped down. The camera person followed suit.

Toklo watched them for a beat longer than necessary.

Then he nodded, impressed despite himself.

"Thought you'd want to stay," he said mildly. "Try to win."

Brittany tightened a strap and glanced up at him, a small, knowing smile tugging at her mouth.

"Yeah," she said. "Well, I learned to respect weather in the mountains in Argentina."

Toklo paused.

Then his eyebrows lifted a fraction.

"I did some hiking in the Andes once," he said. "Wind kicks up fast there. No warning."

Brittany blinked.

Actually blinked.

That... surprised her.

And then she immediately scolded herself for being surprised.

Toklo caught the expression and laughed—short, sharp, genuinely amused.

"We do have planes and shit here, you know," he said, grinning now. "And we do travel places."

Brittany flushed, mortified and laughing at herself.

"Sorry," she said quickly. "Too many *Winterland Who's Who* videos in my childhood."

Toklo barked out a laugh, loud and unrestrained, the sound cutting clean through the wind.

"Those videos lie," he said. "A lot."

Jonah smiled quietly as they hauled the sled into motion, the storm still distant but closing fast.

For the first time since stepping onto the ice, Brittany felt something settle.

Not safety.

But trust.

The sky darkened fast enough to feel personal.

Not a gradual dimming, but a bruising spread of charcoal clouds rolling low and heavy across the horizon, swallowing the light as the wind sharpened into something angrier. Toklo adjusted his course without hesitation.

They were moving fast.

The engine roared beneath them, vibrations traveling up through Brittany's boots and into her bones. The world narrowed to motion and sound and the growing sense that the storm was not interested in waiting.

Toklo's voice crackled through the mic system in their helmets.

"We're not going to make it back to the production house," he said calmly, like he was announcing a change in dinner plans.

Brittany's stomach dipped.

"So where are we going?" Jonah asked, voice steady but alert.

Toklo didn't slow. "My family's place," he replied. "It's not much, but it'll get us through the storm."

Brittany leaned forward and squeezed his shoulder, gratitude sharp and immediate.

"Thank you," she said simply.

Toklo nodded once and pushed the 4x4 harder.

Not much, it turned out, was a bit of a lie.

They crested a rise and the land opened up into a small town nestled against the white expanse. Prefab houses dotted the snow like anchored ships, smoke already curling from vents and chimneys as the wind howled through the streets.

As they approached, a kennel full of huskies erupted into noise—howls and barks rising together in wild harmony, a sound so alive it cut straight through the storm.

Brittany's eyes widened despite herself.

The wind screamed louder now, gusts slamming into them with real force. Toklo veered sharply and hit a small button on the sun visor.

A garage door slid open along the side of a house, and he drove them straight inside as the first heavy flakes began to fall sideways.

The door shut behind them with a solid, comforting thud.

Silence.

Well—relative silence.

Toklo killed the engine and swung off the Skidoo, already reaching to help them down.

"My wife is going to be pissed," he said mildly. "Sorry."

Jonah blinked. "For... the storm?"

Toklo grinned. "For bringing guests."

They followed him into a small mudroom, peeling off layers as heat wrapped around them like a blessing. Gloves. Helmets. Goggles. Boots lined neatly by the wall.

The camera person introduced himself as Steve and thanked Toklo for taking them in. Jonah and Brittany followed suit.

Then the door burst open.

Three small bodies launched themselves at Toklo at once.

"APA!" one shouted. "YOU'RE HOME!" another cried. A third simply wrapped around his leg like a determined koala.

Toklo laughed, real and loud, crouching to gather them up with practiced ease.

"Hey, hey—easy," he said, ruffling hair, accepting hugs, absorbing chaos like this was the best part of his day.

From the kitchen, an attractive Inuit woman looked up from the table where she'd been chopping vegetables.

Her surprise lasted exactly half a second.

Then her expression darkened.

She said something sharp and rapid in a language neither Jonah nor Brittany recognized—but Toklo definitely did.

"Sorry," he replied immediately, tone all apology and charm. "Storm."

Jonah stepped forward awkwardly. "Uh—sorry to barge in—"

The woman narrowed her eyes at him.

Then, slowly, deliberately, she raked her gaze from Jonah's snow-dusted hair down to his broad shoulders, fitted sweater, and very well-put-together form.

She said something else to Toklo.

This time, it *definitely* sounded dirty.

Toklo barked out a laugh, leaned in, and kissed her—quick, familiar, full of affection.

"Steve, Brittany and Jonah," he said, grinning now. "This is my wife, Mary. And these are our kids—Nuna, Ila, and Adlartok."

Mary gave them a single nod, eyes still amused.

"These are our storm guests," Toklo added.

The kids immediately swarmed Brittany and Jonah, questions flying in rapid succession.

"Why are you here?" "Are you famous?" "Did you ride the in the 4x4?" "Are you staying for dinner?"

Brittany laughed, warmth blooming in her chest despite the storm rattling the house.

Whatever was happening outside—

They were safe here.

Sacred Traditions

"Storm guests are a sacred tradition," Mary said, rising from the table and carrying the chopped vegetables to the stove. She tipped them into the pot with a practiced flick of her wrist.

Jonah brightened, eager. "Really?"

Mary snorted.

"No," she said flatly. "Not everything is sacred or traditional, you know."

She shot him a sideways look, lips twitching.

"We're just normal people who live in the cold."

Jonah froze, heat flooding his face. "I—yeah. I know. I mean—" He stumbled, then sighed. "We're fed all sorts of... stories about what it's like to live in up north. I get it."

Mary paused, glanced at him properly this time, and something in her expression softened. The edge faded, replaced by warmth and humour instead of testiness.

"Well," she said lightly, stirring the pot, "if all the men down south are tall and built like you, I might have to move."

Jonah flushed instantly.

This one was deeper. Warmer. Less mortified, more caught.

"Oh," he managed, somewhere between flattered and flustered.

Steve and Brittany burst out laughing.

Toklo did too, leaning back against the counter, clearly enjoying himself.

Mary smiled to herself, satisfied, and went back to her cooking like she hadn't just casually upended Jonah's sense of equilibrium.

The kids laughed along, loud and delighted, even though they had absolutely no idea why.

"Why are we laughing?" Nuna asked.

"Because Dad's friend is red," Ila announced helpfully.

Jonah covered his face with one hand.

Brittany wiped her eyes, still grinning. "For the record," she said, "this is his normal reaction to unexpected flirting."

Mary hummed. "Good to know."

Toklo chuckled. "He'll survive."

The room felt warm now. Lived in. Loud in the good way.

Outside, the wind rattled the walls.

Inside, laughter stuck.

"I thought you were around our age," Brittany said, genuinely puzzled, as she accepted the beer Toklo handed her.

He passed one to Jonah as well, then shrugged like this was hardly worth discussing.

"I am," he said. "Twenty-six."

Brittany blinked.

She looked at him. Then at Mary. Then at the three children orbiting the kitchen like cheerful satellites. The oldest—Nuna—couldn't be younger than seven. Maybe eight.

Her brows knit together as she did the math.

Toklo caught the look and huffed out a short, wry laugh. "There's not a lot to do up here in the winter."

Mary barked out a laugh from across the room and crossed over just as Toklo dropped into a chair at the kitchen table. Without hesitation, she perched sideways on his lap like it was the most natural thing in the world.

"We always find ways to stay warm," she said, voice low and rich with affection.

Toklo's hands came automatically to her waist, fingers splaying there with ease and familiarity. Then—without thinking—his touch lingered. Paused. Softened.

His gaze dropped.

Just for a moment.

But it was enough.

Something in his expression shifted, gentling in a way that made Brittany's chest tighten unexpectedly. Mary followed his eyes and smiled, small and knowing, resting her forehead briefly against his.

Brittany felt it then.

Not suspicion. Not assumption.

Certainty.

Mary was pregnant again.

The realization settled deep in her bones, heavy and warm all at once. The way they moved together. The way the house felt full even in the quiet moments. The way love here wasn't loud or performative—it was lived-in. Constant. Assumed.

Brittany took a slow sip of her beer and let the warmth spread.

She felt it keenly then—not envy exactly, but longing.

This.

This kind of life. This kind of love. Built in layers. Weathered. Real.

Jonah caught her looking, something unreadable flickering across his face before he masked it with a small smile.

The wind rattled the windows again, but inside the kitchen it felt steady. Anchored.

And Brittany wondered—quietly, fiercely—if she would ever find her way to something like this.

Smart Choices

Mary sat for another minute, listening to the rhythm of the house—the wind outside, the pot simmering, the kids humming with pent-up energy—then clapped her hands once.

"Okay," she said briskly. "All of you—out of my kitchen."

The kids groaned in unison.

"I've got to figure out how to make this food stretch for three more guests," Mary continued, shooing them toward the hallway. "Which means less commentary and more space."

She winked at Brittany as she said it, then hooked a finger at Toklo. "Escort service. Now."

Toklo rose obediently, herding children and guests alike toward the living room like this was a well-rehearsed maneuver.

Jonah lingered a half-step behind, awkward and polite. "Do you—uh—need any help?"

Mary glanced over her shoulder, smiling sweetly.

"No, thank you," she said. Then, as if it were an afterthought, added, "Also, second trimester always makes me... what's the word..."

She tilted her head, considering.

"Randy."

Jonah froze.

Mary's eyes flicked pointedly over his broad shoulders, his fitted sweater, the whole very-put-together situation.

"And you looking like *you*," she continued lightly, "well—Toklo might have to shoot you if you stay in here with me by yourself."

Jonah turned the colour of a ripe tomato again.

"Yes. Yep. Living room," he said quickly, backing away like this was now a matter of personal safety.

Toklo snorted as he steered him out. "Smart choice."

The living room was a revelation.

Warm. Lived-in. Soft couches layered with blankets. Shelves crowded with books, board games, and toys in every imaginable shape and colour. A low lamp cast a golden glow that made the storm outside feel very far away.

Brittany was already settled on the couch. Steve grabbed a spot on the floor.

Ila sat beside her, solemn and serious as Brittany gently worked a braid into her dark hair. Adlartok had climbed directly into Brittany's lap, heavy and content, head resting against her chest like he'd known her forever.

Nuna stood in front of them, holding a picture book open and narrating with dramatic flair.

"And *then* the fox said—" he paused, eyes darting to the illustration, "—something very clever."

"Obviously," Brittany agreed seriously, tightening the braid just right. "Foxes are known for that."

Nuna beamed and continued his story with renewed confidence.

Jonah stopped just inside the doorway.

Something in his chest shifted.

The storm howled outside. The house creaked and settled around them. And there was Brittany—laughing softly, patient, surrounded by children like this was the most natural place in the world for her to be.

He swallowed and sat down quietly, not wanting to break the spell.

Jonah was just about to sit when the sound hit them.

Not one engine.

Many.

The distant growl of Skidoos rolled through the little town, growing louder by the second until it threaded through the walls and rattled faintly in the windows.

Toklo didn't even flinch.

"Probably the rest of your show," he said dryly, already pushing himself up from the chair.

Brittany winced. "I'm sorry."

Toklo waved it off as he headed for the door. "I'll go see if they need help."

Jonah stood instinctively. "Do you want some company?"

Toklo paused, then turned back with a small, knowing smile.

"No," he said gently. "You don't know the people here."

He shrugged into his coat, practical and unbothered.

"And your friends are going to need introductions if they want a place to stay that isn't with the dogs."

His grin turned cheeky. Wise. The kind of humour that came from knowing exactly how things worked.

"Stay here in the warmth," he added. "And don't let my kids bug you too much."

Jonah nodded, suddenly aware that this was not a suggestion.

"Got it."

Toklo slipped out into the storm just as the engines drew closer.

Jonah sat down beside Brittany on the couch, close enough that their knees brushed. She didn't move away. Neither did he.

The room settled again.

Nuna, who had been observing them with the intensity of a tiny judge, tilted his head.

"You're married, huh?"

Brittany's face went hot instantly.

"No," she said quickly. "No, we're not."

Jonah glanced at her, lips twitching.

"Not yet anyway."

Brittany turned so fast she nearly knocked into him.

Nuna's face lit up like he'd just been handed a secret.

He leapt off the rug and shouted toward the kitchen, "MA! There's going to be a wedding! You have to marry them!"

Mary appeared in the doorway, wiping her hands on a towel, eyebrow already raised.

"Marry them?" she repeated thoughtfully. "Like I did for Simon and Lula?"

Nuna nodded furiously. "Yes!"

Mary considered this for a beat.

"Okay," she said cheerfully. "After dinner."

Brittany's eyes went *huge*.

Jonah choked on absolutely nothing.

Mary leaned closer, lowering her voice conspiratorially.

"Relax," she said. "Those are Ila's dolls."

She gestured vaguely toward the toy-strewn floor.

"I marry them about once a week. Father JP gives a sermon on living in sin and the kids took it to heart."

Brittany let out a laugh that sounded suspiciously like relief.

Jonah buried his face in his hands.

The kids giggled.

The storm howled outside.

Inside, something warm and ridiculous and unexpectedly tender settled into place.

More Guests

Toklo came back in with the cold clinging to him—and two familiar silhouettes in tow.

"More sacred guests," he announced dryly as he shut the door behind them.

Mary didn't even look up from the stove.

She cackled.

"Oh good," she said. "Just what every peaceful storm shelter needs."

Toklo held up a foil-covered casserole dish like a peace offering. "From Kirima."

Mary's expression softened instantly. She crossed the kitchen, accepted it with exaggerated reverence, and popped it straight into the oven.

"Well then," she said. "I suppose we'll survive."

She glanced over her shoulder at Toklo, eyes dancing. "Do we have to share?"

He leaned in and kissed her quickly, familiar and affectionate. "Yes," he said. "But you can have my share."

Mary giggled and kissed him back, entirely unconcerned with the audience.

Janessa cleared her throat.

Loudly.

Trevor rocked back on his heels, taking in the room with open curiosity. "Wow," he said. "This is... actually really nice."

Mary turned, assessing them with the same sharp efficiency she'd applied to Jonah earlier. Janessa stiffened under the scrutiny, chin lifting instinctively.

Toklo clapped his hands once, reclaiming the moment.

"Come on," he said, steering them toward the living room. "Warmth's in here."

Janessa's eyes flicked over the toys, the blankets, Brittany on the couch with the kids, Jonah beside her. Steve sitting on the floor. Something unreadable passed across her face—surprise, maybe. Or recalculation.

Trevor smiled. "This beats the dogs."

"Barely," Toklo replied.

The door closed behind them, and the house absorbed the newcomers without ceremony.

Outside, the storm howled louder.

Inside, life simply made room.

Toklo ushered Janessa and Trevor into the living room and gestured vaguely at the couches and floor like this was a perfectly normal way to acquire houseguests during a storm.

"Sit," he said. "Or don't."

Janessa hesitated, clearly recalculating her place in a room that did not care about her storyline.

Trevor dropped onto the rug, already reaching for a stray toy truck like it had been waiting just for him.

"This is cozy," he said sincerely. "Ten out of ten storm vibes."

Mary's voice floated in from the kitchen. "Don't get comfortable. Everyone eats. Then we reassess life choices."

The kids cheered.

Janessa perched stiffly on the edge of an armchair, hands folded in her lap, scanning the room like she was trying to identify who the alpha was. Her gaze snagged on Brittany, surrounded by children, relaxed and laughing.

Something flickered in Janessa's eyes.

Brittany caught it—and then deliberately looked away.

Nuna plopped down on the floor between Jonah and Brittany, legs crossed. "Are you really going to get married?" he asked, voice loud enough to carry.

Janessa's head snapped around.

Brittany opened her mouth.

Jonah beat her to it. "We're... discussing it."

Brittany shot him a look.

Trevor choked on a laugh.

Janessa stared between them, visibly glitching.

Mary leaned against the counter, arms crossed, observing everything with a satisfied air. "I'll need at least two witnesses and someone willing to hold the dolls."

"I volunteer!" Ila shouted.

Adlartok climbed onto Jonah's knee without asking and began investigating his watch.

Janessa blinked again. "Okay," she said slowly. "So... this is happening."

Toklo shrugged. "Storms bring people together."

Mary smirked. "Sometimes against their will."

The wind slammed into the house, rattling the windows hard enough to make everyone jump.

Toklo glanced toward the door. "Good thing you're all here. Would've been a long night with just us."

Brittany felt Jonah's knee press lightly against hers. Steady. Present.

She didn't move away.

Janessa folded her arms, lips pressing into a thin line as she watched the room settle around Brittany and Jonah like they belonged there.

And for the first time since the storm started, Brittany realized something important.

This space wasn't loud. It wasn't competitive. It wasn't performative.

It was *real*.

And Janessa had no idea how to exist inside it.

Family Dinner

Mary clapped her hands once, sharp and decisive.

"Dinner," she called. "Before I lose my patience or someone eats a crayon."

That was apparently the cue.

Toklo disappeared briefly and returned with a mismatched collection of chairs scavenged from other rooms, setting them around the table with easy efficiency. No ceremony. No fuss. Just the practiced choreography of a house used to making room.

The food hit the table in steaming bowls.

The casserole from Kirima turned out to be a fish stew, rich and fragrant, the fish so tender it fell apart at the touch of a spoon. Potatoes soaked up the broth, onions melted into sweetness, and the whole thing tasted like warmth and salt and care.

Brittany closed her eyes on the first bite.

"Oh wow," she murmured.

Toklo grinned, clearly pleased.

He cracked open another beer and poured it into smaller glasses so everyone could share, sliding them across the table like this was a celebration instead of an emergency shelter.

The kids wasted no time.

"So what's the show about?" Nuna asked, mouth already full.

"Do people fight?" Ila demanded.

"Is there kissing?" Adlartok asked, hopeful.

Trevor laughed and took it upon himself to answer, spinning a version of events that leaned heavily into the ridiculous. He talked about bad challenges, worse costumes, people slipping on ice, and producers who took things way too seriously.

He left out the jealousy. The spirals. The sharp edges.

Nuna laughed so hard he tipped backward in his chair and landed on the floor with a thump, cackling.

Mary didn't even look up. "If you're alive, get up."

Nuna did, still laughing.

Jonah found himself smiling without effort, watching Brittany eat, relaxed and flushed from the warmth. Watching Trevor with the kids, unexpectedly gentle. Watching Toklo and Mary exchange quiet glances that said *this is good.*

Even Janessa loosened.

She laughed at one of Trevor's stories, surprised by the sound of it herself, shoulders finally dropping as she took another spoonful of stew. For once, she wasn't performing. Just... present.

Outside, the storm battered the house.

Inside, there was food. Laughter. Full mouths and empty bowls.

And for a while, it felt like everyone belonged.

After dinner, Trevor surprised everyone by stacking plates and rolling up his sleeves.

"I've got dishes," he announced easily.

Janessa blinked.

Then, just as surprising, she stood. "I'll dry."

The room paused for half a beat, recalibrating.

Brittany exchanged a glance with Jonah.

Huh.

They watched from the doorway as Trevor worked methodically at the sink, humming under his breath, while Janessa dried and handed plates back with quiet efficiency. No sniping. No theatrics. Just... teamwork.

Brittany felt something shift.

Maybe she'd underestimated them. Or maybe people were more than the roles they played when cameras were hungry.

Jonah leaned close. "Add that to the list of unexpected plot twists."

She nodded. "Right under 'storm shelter marriage.'"

As if summoned by the words, Mary clapped her hands.

"Okay," she announced. "Ceremony time."

The kids erupted.

Nuna dragged out a plastic tiara. Ila produced a scarf that had clearly lived many lives as a wedding veil. Adlartok solemnly handed Jonah a spoon.

"For vows," he explained.

Mary stood at the front of the living room, a dish towel draped over one shoulder like ceremonial regalia.

"We gather today," she began, deadpan, "because a storm said so."

Toklo snorted. Steve laughed out loud.

Brittany laughed, then caught herself. Something in Mary's voice had softened, grounding the joke without stripping it of meaning.

She spoke about choosing kindness. About shelter. About not knowing where you'll land, but showing up anyway.

It was silly.

And somehow… beautiful.

Brittany felt Jonah's attention beside her, steady and warm.

"Do you promise," Mary asked, "to face storms together. Or at least not abandon each other for the dogs."

"I do," Jonah said, smiling.

"I do," Brittany echoed, surprised by the weight of the words even as she laughed.

The kids clapped wildly.

"And now," Mary said, "you seal it with a kiss."

Brittany turned toward Jonah, already bracing herself to make it light. Playful. Barely-there.

Just enough to satisfy the audience of children.

Their lips touched.

Soft. Brief. Almost nothing.

Except—

It wasn't nothing.

It rolled through her like a spark down a wire, quick and undeniable, settling somewhere deep and warm. Her breath caught. Her toes curled inside her socks.

Jonah stilled, just for a fraction of a second, like he felt it too.

Then they pulled back.

The kids cheered.

Trevor whooped. Steve clapped.

Janessa smiled, something unreadable flickering behind her eyes.

Brittany laughed a little too loudly.

But inside, something had shifted.

And she knew—absolutely knew—that wasn't the kind of kiss you could forget.

Bedtime

Outside, the wind howled like it had something personal to say.

The house creaked and groaned under the pressure, the storm throwing itself against the walls in long, relentless gusts. Ice rattled against the windows, and somewhere nearby the huskies answered back, their voices rising and falling in wild harmony.

Toklo moved through the house with calm efficiency, assigning sleeping arrangements like this was a perfectly ordinary end to a perfectly ordinary day.

"Okay," he said, gesturing down the hall. "Brittany. Janessa. Kids' room."

Janessa nodded quickly, clearly relieved not to argue.

Toklo turned. "Trevor. Jonah. Other room. Steve, you're on the couch."

Jonah blinked. "That's... fine."

Trevor grinned. "I've shared worse."

The kids, already half-asleep from the excitement and full bellies, had been deposited into their parents' room without protest. Mary disappeared briefly and returned with an armful of folded clothes.

"Sleepwear," she announced. "Best I can do on short notice."

She handed out shirts and sweatpants to the men and sleep shirts to the women.

They were... optimistic in their sizing.

Jonah stared at the shirt. "This is for... a child?"

Mary smiled sweetly. "A very beloved child."

Trevor went into the bathroom and pulled his on without hesitation. The hem stopped well above his waist. Jonah followed suit, the fabric stretching valiantly across his shoulders before surrendering entirely.

Both men were left standing there in too-short sweatpants and shirts that revealed a frankly disrespectful amount of stomach.

Mary froze.

Her eyes flicked up.

Then very deliberately away.

Then back again.

"Oh," she said, clearing her throat. "Right. Yes. Okay. Everyone's... covered."

Toklo didn't even look surprised. He just shook his head slowly.

"Too bad the kids are sleeping with us tonight," he said quietly to his wife.

The timing was unfortunate.

The volume was not.

Mary turned bright red and burst into laughter at the same time, clapping a hand over her mouth.

Trevor snorted.

Jonah covered his face.

From the hallway, Brittany let out a helpless laugh, while Janessa muttered, "I walked into *this*."

Toklo kissed Mary's temple, still smiling. "Storm's long. Night's young."

Mary swatted his arm. "Go put the men away before I make bad decisions."

The wind howled again, louder this time.

The house, warm and full and entirely too alive, settled in for the night.

Later, as Jonah lay in bed, he told himself it was a joke.

A storm thing. A kids thing. A Mary-with-a-dish-towel thing.

He had stood there smiling, holding a spoon like a prop, surrounded by laughter and plastic tiaras and a woman who had married dolls more times than she could count, and he kept telling himself none of it mattered.

Except it did.

It mattered the moment Mary said *we gather today* and his chest tightened for reasons that made no sense. It mattered when Brittany said *I do* with that half-laugh, half-brace in her voice, like she was trying to keep the words from rooting too deeply.

It mattered when the kids clapped and the room felt warmer, fuller, like it had decided something without asking them.

And then Mary said it.

"Seal it with a kiss."

Jonah turned to Brittany, already preparing himself to keep it light. Quick. Polite. A peck that would make everyone laugh and move on.

She looked up at him.

Her eyes were bright, a little uncertain, a little daring. Close enough that he could see the faint flush on her cheeks, the way her breath hitched once before she leaned in.

Their lips touched.

Soft. Brief. Barely there.

And Jonah's world tilted.

It wasn't the kind of kiss that stole your breath or made fireworks explode. It was worse than that.

It was familiar.

It felt like recognition. Like something slipping into place after being misaligned for far too long. Warmth spread through him, deep and steady, not sharp or urgent but grounding in a way that made his hands curl reflexively at his sides.

He stilled.

Just for a heartbeat.

Because if he moved—if he leaned in, if he let himself respond the way every nerve in his body wanted to—this would stop being a joke.

Brittany pulled back first.

The room erupted in cheers. Laughter. Clapping. Someone yelled *again!* and someone else dropped a toy.

Jonah smiled because smiling was expected.

But inside, everything had gone quiet.

That ceremony had felt more real than it had any right to.

More real than the show. More real than the cameras. More real than anything he'd let himself imagine lately.

He had glanced at Brittany, searching her face for confirmation that he wasn't alone in feeling it.

She laughed too loud. Looked away too quickly.

And Jonah understood.

Whatever that was—it wasn't something she was ready to name.

So he tucked the feeling away carefully, like something precious and dangerous.

And told himself it was just a kiss.

Flashbacks

That night, as sleep finally crept in, it didn't come gently.

It came sideways.

Brittany drifted under and found herself somewhere else entirely—back in a different room, a different dark, a different kind of storm pressing in around her.

The night before her mother died.

The house had been too quiet then. Like it already knew. The air heavy with that unbearable waiting, every sound amplified, every breath a reminder that time was running out.

She remembered sitting on the edge of the bed, hands twisted together, heart pounding like it was trying to outrun the inevitable. She hadn't been brave. She hadn't been strong.

She had been terrified.

Jonah had been there.

Of course he had.

He always was.

She remembered how she'd clung to him, fingers digging into the fabric of his shirt like he was the only solid thing left in a world that was already breaking apart. They both knew it was the end. No pretending. No soft lies.

She couldn't do it alone.

And he hadn't let her.

They'd spent the night together—not rushed, not desperate, but aching in that quiet way that comes when love and grief collide. When touch isn't about want so much as survival.

He'd held her like he meant it.

Like it was a vow.

She could still hear his voice, low and sure in the dark, promising her things she hadn't even known she needed to hear.

That this wasn't just comfort. That this wasn't just grief. That this was the beginning of something.

He told her he'd always loved her.

That they were real.

That no matter what happened next, he wasn't going anywhere. That he would never let her go.

And for one fragile, dangerous moment—she had believed him.

Then her life fell apart.

Her mother was gone. Her father, collected her and she disappeared into a life off the grid in Argentina, unreachable in every way that mattered. Phones didn't work. Addresses dissolved. Distance became absolute.

In her bones, Brittany knew the truth even then—that contact would have been impossible.

But hope is stubborn.

For years, she carried it anyway.

A quiet, aching hope that maybe one day she'd hear from him. That maybe something solid would emerge from the wreckage. That maybe Jonah's promise hadn't been swallowed whole by grief and chaos and time.

She held onto it longer than she should have.

Until one day she didn't anymore.

And that loss—quiet, unmarked, and deeply personal—hurt almost as much as the first.

As Brittany slept, the memory faded, leaving behind the ache it always did.

Unresolved. Unfinished. Still alive.

Storm Logic

Morning didn't arrive so much as *announce itself.*

The wind was still howling, relentless and insistent, rattling the walls and shaking snow loose from the roof in soft avalanches that thudded against the side of the house. The storm hadn't moved on in the night. If anything, it had settled in.

Which, apparently, meant it was time to throw a party.

"Well," Mary said cheerfully, pulling on her boots, "if you can't go anywhere, you might as well feed everyone and let them sing."

Brittany blinked, still half-asleep. "Is that... a thing?"

Toklo shrugged. "Storm logic."

By the time they bundled up and made their way across the small town to the church, the entire town seemed to have had the same idea.

The community room buzzed with energy, the kind that comes from shared inconvenience turned into shared purpose. Long tables were being set up. Massive pots appeared like magic. Someone had already started a fire going in the big stove at the back.

The town was small—about a hundred people on a good day.

With the film crew and cast folded in, it swelled to nearly a hundred and twenty, and somehow that made it feel more alive, not less. Like the storm had shaken the place and everything loose had landed together.

The crew set up quietly in the background, capturing "B-roll" and setting up the actual church confessional as the show confessional booth.

Mary handed Brittany a knife and a crate of potatoes. “You chop.”

“Yes, ma’am,” Brittany said, smiling despite herself.

Jonah found himself wrangling toddlers with Trevor, building an elaborate tower out of blocks while being aggressively instructed by a five-year-old named Eli who took his architectural authority very seriously.

“No, no,” Eli said patiently. “That one goes *there* or it falls.”

Jonah nodded solemnly. “I appreciate the guidance.”

Janessa hovered at first, clearly unsure what role to play when there were no cameras demanding reaction shots. Eventually, she was handed a tray of Bannock dough and a chair beside an older woman who told her exactly how to knead it.

“You’ll know when it’s ready,” the woman said. “It stops fighting you.”

Janessa laughed—quiet, surprised. “I relate to that.”

As the morning wore on, the room shifted again.

Someone suggested games.

Then someone else suggested a talent show.

And suddenly there was a sign-up sheet taped to the wall, kids arguing about song choices, adults groaning theatrically about *absolutely not* while secretly practicing in corners.

Brittany found herself laughing more than she had in weeks.

The storm still screamed outside, but in here there was music, clapping, the smell of food, and the low hum of people choosing joy because there were no other options.

She caught Jonah watching her from across the room, something soft and steady in his expression.

She looked away before it could mean too much.

But she didn’t feel like running.

The talent show was exactly what it sounded like.

Chaotic. Unfiltered. Perfect.

Someone had dragged a crooked little stage out from the storage room. Someone else had found a microphone that only worked if you held it at a very specific angle and whispered encouragement into it first. Kids argued loudly over whose turn it was. Adults swore they were *absolutely not participating* while being aggressively signed up by their neighbours.

There was a recorder solo that tested the limits of human patience. A dramatic reading of a grocery list. Two teenagers who performed a dance that ended in laughter and applause because no one fell.

The storm raged outside, but inside the church the noise was joyful and messy and alive.

Mary was halfway through laughing at something one of the kids had said when Toklo stood up.

The room went quiet.

Not because anyone expected anything special—Toklo just had that kind of presence. Calm. Grounded. The sort of man who didn't waste words and never took the floor without a reason.

He cleared his throat and took the microphone.

Mary tilted her head. "What are you doing?"

Toklo smiled at her. Not playful. Not teasing.

Soft.

"For you," he said simply.

Someone strummed a guitar.

Then Toklo sang.

His voice was deep and steady, richer than anyone expected, filling the room with a warmth that cut straight through the chatter and landed somewhere tender. He sang **The Way You Look Tonight**, every word aimed squarely at Mary, who froze mid-laugh and stared at him like she'd just discovered something entirely new about the man she loved.

He didn't perform.

He *offered* it.

Mary's hand flew to her mouth. Her eyes went glossy. The room faded away as Toklo sang like the world had narrowed to one woman sitting in a folding chair, pregnant and radiant and utterly undone.

By the time he finished, the room was silent.

Then Mary stood up, walked straight to him, and kissed him like she'd waited all day to do it.

The church exploded.

Cheers. Whistles. Kids screaming. Someone shouted, "DO IT AGAIN."

Mary laughed and pressed her forehead to Toklo's. "I married you for reasons," she said thickly. "This is one of them."

Brittany felt it in her chest, sharp and sweet all at once. The kind of love that didn't need explaining. The kind that grew quietly and then filled rooms.

She glanced at Jonah.

He wasn't looking at the stage anymore.

He was looking at her.

And suddenly the storm outside felt very, very far away.

A Moment

Brittany turned away too fast.

The room was still buzzing with applause, laughter, the echo of Toklo's voice wrapped around Mary like a promise kept—but it hit Brittany wrong. Too close. Too familiar. Too much like the night her life split open and never quite sealed again.

The dream from last night surged up without warning.

The safety. The grief. And the abandonment.

Her chest tightened.

She grabbed her coat off the back of a chair and slipped out before anyone could stop her, before she had to explain why her hands were shaking or why her throat felt like it was closing in on itself.

Outside, the wind was brutal.

It tore at her coat, bit through her gloves, stole the breath straight from her lungs. Snow stung her cheeks as she walked a few steps away from the church, head bowed, shoulders hunched.

She needed a moment.

Just a minute. Less than that.

The cold didn't numb the ache. It sharpened it.

She didn't realize she was crying until the tears froze against her skin, lashes clumping together, her breath hitching in short, ugly pulls.

The door opened behind her.

"Britt?"

Jonah's voice was nearly swallowed by the wind, carried to her in fragments.

She closed her eyes.

Too late.

She turned as he came closer, close enough now that she could see his face, tight with concern, hair already dusted white with snow.

"Don't, Jonah—" she started, the words breaking as soon as they left her mouth.

He stopped in front of her, scanning her face like he was trying to understand damage he couldn't see.

"What's wrong?" he asked.

And then, softer. "What did I do?"

Something in his voice gave way on that last question. It wasn't defensive. It wasn't angry.

It was hurt.

Like she'd taken something fragile and cracked it without meaning to.

Her hands curled into fists at her sides.

She hadn't planned this. She hadn't rehearsed it. But once the truth pressed up against her ribs, there was no shoving it back down.

"You never came," she said.

The words were quiet.

They landed anyway.

Jonah stilled.

"You said you weren't going to leave me alone," she continued, voice shaking now, years of restraint dissolving all at once. "I know it's dumb. We were kids. I *know* that."

Her breath hitched hard.

"But you promised."

The wind roared around them, but Jonah didn't move. Didn't interrupt. His face had gone pale, like something inside him had just dropped out.

"And then—" Brittany swallowed, pain flaring sharp and hot through the cold, "then you weren't there when I needed you."

Her voice cracked completely on the last word.

She looked at him then, really looked, and the past and present tangled together so tightly she couldn't tell where one ended.

"I waited," she said. "I waited longer than I should have."

Silence stretched between them, heavy and merciless.

The storm howled.

And Brittany stood there shaking, finally having said the thing she'd carried like a stone in her chest for years.

Jonah didn't speak right away.

The wind tore at his coat, rattled his breath, pushed snow between them like it wanted a say in the conversation. He stood there, eyes on Brittany, like he was deciding whether to bleed out loud.

Finally, he exhaled.

"I thought we'd have a few days," he said quietly. "At least."

His voice was rough now, worn thin by memory.

"I had my mom make up the spare room for you," he went on. "Clean sheets. Extra blankets. I told her you might need somewhere quiet. Somewhere safe."

Brittany's chest tightened.

"I thought you'd be there when I got to your place," he said, swallowing hard. "I thought I'd open the door and you'd be there. Or you'd come back. Or someone would know where you were."

His hands curled, then stilled, like he was gripping something invisible.

"But you weren't."

His voice cracked, just barely.

"There was no one," he said. "Nothing. The house was empty. Quiet in a way that felt wrong."

He shook his head once, slow and disbelieving even now.

"My parents called CPS," he continued. "They said your dad had taken you to Argentina."

Brittany flinched.

"I tried, Britt," Jonah said, the words coming faster now, urgency bleeding through his restraint. "I really did. I asked questions. I made calls. I followed every thread anyone gave me."

His eyes lifted to hers, raw and open.

"But it was like your dad didn't want to be found," he said. "No address. No phone. No trail that led anywhere solid."

The wind howled, filling the space where his breath hitched.

"And I didn't know how to keep looking without anything," he finished softly. "Not without a name, or a place, or someone telling me where to start."

Silence fell again.

Not empty this time.

Heavy. Shared.

Jonah looked at her like he'd been carrying this explanation for years, waiting for the moment she'd finally ask.

"I never stopped thinking about you," he said, quieter now. "But I didn't know how to reach you."

The storm raged on.

But something between them had shifted—pain still there, still sharp—but no longer unanswered.

Unexpected Truth

Brittany didn't answer right away.

The storm filled the silence for her, wind screaming across the snow like it was furious on her behalf. She stared at Jonah, at the earnest lines of his face, the way his shoulders were braced like he was ready to take whatever she threw next.

She hadn't expected this.

She'd expected excuses. Or defensiveness. Or a shrug and a *we were young* that would make her feel foolish for still carrying it.

Instead, he'd given her a room she'd never slept in.

She swallowed.

"I didn't know any of that," she said finally, and her voice came out thin, scraped raw. "I didn't know you looked. I didn't know you tried."

Jonah nodded once, like he didn't deserve anything more than that.

"I know," he said.

That did something to her.

The acceptance. The lack of demand. The way he didn't rush in to claim forgiveness like it was owed to him.

"I thought you chose not to," she whispered. "I thought you decided I was... too much. That grief made me unlovable."

Her breath caught, sharp and painful.

"So I built a whole story around that," she went on. "I carried it with me. Everywhere. I told myself you left because people always leave when things get hard."

Jonah's jaw tightened. His eyes went glossy, but he didn't interrupt.

"I needed that story," Brittany said, voice breaking now. "Because the alternative—that everything just fell apart without anyone being able to stop it—felt worse."

The wind gusted harder, shoving at her back. Jonah stepped closer instinctively, not touching, just blocking the worst of it.

"I didn't want to believe you tried," she admitted. "Because then I would've had to sit with the idea that we both lost each other."

She looked up at him then.

"That it wasn't abandonment," she said. "It was... chaos."

Jonah let out a shaky breath.

"I don't need you to forgive me," he said quietly. "I just need you to know I never chose to disappear."

Something in Brittany's chest loosened. Not all the way. But enough to breathe.

"I don't know what to do with this yet," she said honestly.

"That's okay," he replied immediately. "You don't have to."

They stood there, close now, the space between them no longer sharp but charged. Jonah lifted a hand halfway, hesitated, then let it fall again.

"I missed you," he said, like it had cost him something to admit it. "Even when I didn't know where you were."

Brittany's eyes burned.

"I missed who I was before everything broke," she said softly. "And you were part of that."

The storm roared on, relentless and unbothered.

But inside that narrow pocket of cold and truth, something fragile and real took shape.

Not a reunion.

Not yet.

But understanding.

And for the first time in years, Brittany didn't feel alone in the memory.

Brittany wasn't sure what she was about to do.

Step closer. Or step back.

She hovered in the space between, weight shifting almost imperceptibly on the snow, breath caught halfway between resolve and retreat. Everything in her felt sharpened by the cold, by the truth they'd just laid bare, by the way Jonah stood there looking at her like she was something fragile and precious all at once.

She didn't trust herself with either option.

Then someone tugged on Jonah's sleeve.

Hard.

Jonah startled, breaking eye contact, and turned just in time to hear a voice carried thinly through the wind. Toklo—his face wrapped in a scarf, eyes wide—said something Brittany couldn't quite make out over the howl of the storm.

Jonah nodded sharply.

When he turned back, he didn't hesitate.

He reached out and caught Brittany's sleeve.

Not her hand. Not her wrist.

Just the edge of her coat, fingers curling into the fabric like a quiet question instead of a demand.

"Storm's getting worse," he said, leaning in so close she could hear him over the wind. His voice brushed her ear, low and urgent. "Toklo says we need to go inside. Now."

His face was inches from hers.

Close enough that she could see the flecks of snow melting in his hair. Close enough to feel the warmth of his breath despite the cold. Close enough that the space between them felt charged and unfinished.

She nodded.

Not trusting her voice.

And instead of pulling away, she let herself be led.

They moved together back toward the church, Jonah walking just ahead of her, his grip still light but steady, like he was making sure she didn't get lost in the whiteout.

The wind roared louder behind them, erasing their footprints almost as soon as they made them.

Brittany didn't look back.

But for the first time in a long while, she let someone guide her through the storm.

And that felt like something.

Community

Brittany followed Jonah and Toklo back into the church, the door shutting behind them with a solid, reassuring thud.

Warmth rushed in immediately—heat, laughter, the low hum of voices overlapping in easy familiarity. The storm raged on outside, but in here there was light and movement and the kind of comfort that came from people who knew how to weather things together.

This was what survival looked like up here. Not silence. Not stoicism.

Community.

Jonah walked a step ahead of her, glancing back more than once, checking on her without making it obvious. His concern didn't grate the way it once might have. It didn't feel like pressure.

It felt like care.

And for once, Brittany didn't flinch from it.

She let the thoughts she'd been holding at bay finally settle, rearranging themselves into something that made sense. What had happened between them back then—it hadn't been imagined. It hadn't been one-sided. It had been something real.

Real enough to hurt this much.

She'd crushed it down because she'd believed the story she needed to survive—that she had been left behind. That loving too deeply had made her disposable.

But now she saw it differently.

Jonah had felt it too.

He had lost her in the same sudden, brutal way. He had carried his own version of the damage forward, quieter maybe, but no less real.

That realization landed hard.

And strangely, gently.

Shit.

That made it all real in a way she hadn't been ready for before.

The anger she'd been nursing so carefully—keeping it alive because it felt safer than grief—began to drain away. Not all at once. Not cleanly. But steadily, like pressure releasing from a wound that had been festering for far too long.

It stung.

But it was also... relief.

Healing, she realized, wasn't a moment. It was permission. To stop bracing. To let things breathe.

Brittany took a slow breath and stepped fully back into the room, into the noise and warmth and imperfect, human mess of it all.

For the first time in years, she wasn't carrying the weight alone.

They shrugged out of their coats near the door, the little entryway already crowded with parkas, scarves, and mittens in every imaginable colour. Hooks were overburdened. Sleeves slid off pegs. Someone's toque fell to the floor and was immediately scooped up and rehung at a jaunty angle.

It was chaos in the most harmless way.

Brittany tried to wedge her coat onto an empty peg, pressing it flat like that might convince gravity to cooperate. It didn't. The coat sagged, slipped, then fell.

She laughed under her breath.

And she let herself feel it.

The normalcy. The smallness. The fact that this was what her body chose to notice after everything that had just cracked open.

She found another peg and hung her coat up properly this time, smoothing it down with quiet determination, like she was staking a claim.

Jonah hung his coat beside hers.

The sight of it—his coat next to hers, fabric brushing fabric—hit her harder than she expected. It felt symbolic in a way she didn't want to overthink, so she didn't.

When he turned to go, she reached out and caught his hand.

Just like that.

Jonah stopped instantly, as if the motion had rewired him mid-step. He looked back at her, concern flashing across his face first—automatic, ingrained—followed by something warmer. Something hopeful. Something that felt dangerously familiar.

Brittany didn't speak.

She just let her lips twitch, the beginnings of a smile she hadn't realized she'd been holding back for years.

And Jonah bloomed.

It was the smile.

The one she'd fallen in love with back then. The one that didn't just curve his mouth but lit up his entire face, eyes bright, posture loosening like he'd been given permission to be exactly who he was.

For a split second, he didn't look like a man carrying old grief and careful restraint.

He looked like a teenager again.

Open. Unarmoured. Hers.

The moment passed quickly—people moving around them, voices rising, the world intruding again—but something had shifted.

The storm still raged outside.

But inside, right there by the coat pegs, Brittany felt steady.

"I don't know what I'm ready for," Brittany said quietly.

Her voice didn't shake, but it wasn't armoured either. It lived somewhere honest in between.

"There's still a lot to figure out," she went on. "But I'm ready for more than being hurt. And angry."

She stepped closer as she spoke, the movement small but deliberate. Around them, coats brushed against each other on the pegs, fabric whispering softly in the draft that slipped in through the doorframe. The wind outside howled like it wanted in on the conversation, cold fingers sneaking through the seams of the building.

Jonah didn't hesitate.

He opened his arms.

Brittany closed the distance and leaned into him, resting her head against his chest like it had always known the way. His warmth soaked through her instantly, steady and grounding. She exhaled, long and slow, letting herself settle.

For the first time in years, she wasn't bracing.

"It was just... shitty all around, huh?" she murmured.

She felt him nod against her forehead, the motion gentle and sure.

"It was," Jonah said. "It really was."

He rested his chin lightly against her hair, his hands warm at her back, not gripping, not claiming. Just holding.

"But this doesn't have to be," he continued, his voice low now, stripped of the careful polish he usually wore. "I know this is TV. I know we're being thrown together because it makes good footage."

His breath hitched slightly, like he was stepping onto thin ice and choosing to trust it anyway.

"But if there's a chance," he said, "that we could see where this goes—really see—then I'll bow out here. No games. No pressure."

Brittany's heart thudded hard against his chest.

"I don't want to do this halfway," Jonah finished softly. "Not with you."

She didn't answer right away.

She stayed where she was, forehead tucked under his chin, listening to the steady beat of his heart and the chaos of the storm beyond the walls.

For the first time, the future didn't feel like something she had to run from.

It felt like something she could step toward.

The Name of the Game

"Jonah," Brittany said, lifting her head just enough to look at him properly, eyes bright with something new and electric. "The name of the game is love."

He stilled.

"So let's go all in instead of out," she continued, voice low but certain. "Let's make the viewers fall in love with love. Then we can have both—the win *and* us."

She paused, just long enough to make him feel the weight of it.

"At least try," she added softly. "What do you think?"

Jonah's heart didn't just speed up.

It *sang*.

He could feel it—right there in his chest—this ridiculous, buoyant lift, like something long dormant had suddenly remembered how to live. He let out a breath that might've been a laugh, might've been relief.

"You, me," he said slowly, warmth threading through his voice, "and a competition where we're actually working together?"

His mouth curved, humour bubbling up now that the fear had loosened its grip.

"You realize that's not going to be remotely fair to everyone else, right?"

Brittany laughed, the sound light and unburdened, like she'd already decided the answer.

"I'm good with it," she said easily. "We've basically been running a classic enemies-to-lovers arc anyway."

She tilted her head, eyes gleaming.

"So what do you say we start with a heated argument," she continued, warming to the idea, "that I end by kissing you. Full-on. In front of the cameras."

Jonah blinked.

Brittany kept going, hands gesturing now like she was mapping out a campaign strategy.

"We get the feminist vote," she said, ticking it off. "The sexy vote. And the redemption arc—all in one."

She smiled, sharp and confident and devastating.

Jonah didn't hesitate.

He nodded once, decisive and utterly undone.

"I'm in."

And this time, there was no fear in it.

Only momentum.

The cameras found them faster than Brittany expected.

Of course they did.

She and Jonah had barely stepped fully back into the body of the room when Steph's head snapped up, eyes narrowing with interest. There was a subtle shift in the air—the barely perceptible tightening that came when story instincts kicked in.

Brittany felt it.

And instead of shrinking, she leaned into it.

She stopped walking.

Jonah took another step before realizing she wasn't beside him anymore. He turned, brows drawing together in mild confusion—and then awareness flickered across his face as he clocked the camera angling toward them.

Brittany crossed her arms.

"Oh, so *now* you're calm?" she said, her voice carrying just enough edge to turn heads. "That's convenient."

Jonah blinked once.

Then, beautifully, he caught up.

"Excuse me?" he asked, tone cool, confused-but-not-defensive. "I've been calm this entire time."

A few people nearby went quiet. Someone's kid stopped banging a spoon on the table.

Brittany scoffed. "Right. Because disappearing for years and then popping back up like this doesn't count as chaos."

Jonah stepped closer, his jaw tightening just enough to sell it.

"You think I wanted that?" he shot back. "You think any of this was my choice?"

The room had gone very still now.

The camera leaned in.

Brittany's heart was pounding—not with fear, but with adrenaline. With intention. With the delicious thrill of choosing her moment.

"You don't get to decide when it matters," she said sharply. "You don't get to rewrite how that felt for me."

Jonah's voice dropped. "And you don't get to pretend it didn't matter to me."

That did it.

Brittany took the final step forward.

"Then stop standing there like you're waiting for permission," she snapped—and before anyone could react, before Jonah could say another word, she grabbed the front of his shirt and kissed him.

Hard.

Decisive.

The kind of kiss that wasn't asking.

Gasps rippled through the room.

The camera operator made a noise that was definitely not professional.

Jonah froze for half a heartbeat—then his hands came up, one settling at her waist, the other under her hair like he was afraid she'd disappear again if he didn't anchor her.

The kiss softened.

Shifted.

Turned into something warm and devastatingly real.

When Brittany pulled back, the room was silent.

She rested her forehead briefly against his, just long enough for the moment to land.

"Next time," she said quietly, "we talk instead of walking away."

Jonah smiled—small, stunned, undone.

"Deal," he murmured.

Somewhere behind them, someone whispered, "Holy shit."

The storm howled outside.

Inside, the story had just caught fire.

Steph Ascending

Steph was already moving.

The second Brittany's hands hit Jonah's shirt and the kiss landed, Steph's brain flipped into full crisis-management mode. She yanked her headset down around her neck and spun in a tight circle, eyes scanning the room like a general assessing a battlefield.

"Okay," she muttered, mostly to herself. "Okay. Okay, that's... that's not bad. That's not bad at all."

A PA skidded to a stop beside her. "Do we... do we cut?"

"No," Steph snapped immediately. "Absolutely not. We *stay* on them. Are you kidding me?"

She jabbed a finger toward the camera operator, who looked like he'd just witnessed the collapse of civilization as he knew it.

"Stay wide," Steph ordered. "Then punch in. I want faces. I want reactions. I want the *room*."

She turned, already barking new instructions. "Get Jonah and Brittany separate confessionals after this. I want it raw. No notes. No warning. And someone—someone please make sure the sound guy didn't faint."

Behind her, the church buzzed with whispers and poorly contained delight. Even the locals looked impressed, which Steph took as an excellent sign.

"This," she said under her breath, eyes gleaming, "is television."

Trevor had no idea where he was until he sat down.

"Wait," he said, glancing around the small wooden booth. "Trevor has to ask—is this... an actual confessional?"

The PA on the other side of the screen grinned. "Yes."

Trevor blinked. "Like... Catholic?"

"Like very," she confirmed. "Talk to me."

Trevor ran a hand through his hair and let out a breath that sounded suspiciously like a laugh.

"Well," he said, leaning back slightly, "Trevor thinks this feels... ironic."

He glanced up at the little lattice screen separating him from the camera.

"Bless me, Father, for I, Trevor, have witnessed absolute chaos," he said solemnly.

The PA snorted.

Trevor shook his head, a smile creeping in despite himself. "Trevor thought this show was going to be about strategy and alliances and who can outlast Trevor."

He paused, expression shifting.

"And then Brittany just—" He made a vague kissing motion with his hand. "—blew the doors off the place."

He leaned forward now, elbows on his knees, voice dropping.

"That wasn't for the cameras," he said slowly. "Trevor has been on enough reality shows to know the difference. Trevor knows that was... personal."

Trevor sighed.

"And honestly?" he continued. "Trevor believes good for them."

He smiled, soft and a little awed.

"Trevor feels that Jonah looked like someone had just handed him something he didn't think he was allowed to want anymore. And Brittany? She looked like she'd finally decided to stop being mad at the wrong version of the story."

He glanced around again, taking in the booth.

"Trevor is sitting in a church confessional talking about love on a reality show," he added. "So clearly the storm has scrambled all of us, including Trevor."

Trevor shrugged.

"But if this is what chaos looks like," he said, grin widening, "Trevor is into it."

Church Confessions

Brittany sat down and immediately crossed her arms.

Not defensive—contained.

The confessional was quieter than she expected. Dimmer. The thick church walls muted the storm outside, turning it into a low, constant presence instead of a roar. She could still hear it, though. You couldn't really escape weather like that.

She exhaled slowly and glanced toward the camera.

"So," she said, lips quirking. "I'm guessing you want to talk about the kiss."

Paige laughed softly from behind the lens. "If you're up for it."

Brittany nodded once. "Yeah. Okay."

She uncrossed her arms, hands folding in her lap like she was bracing herself for honesty.

"I didn't plan it the way it looked," she admitted. "I mean—yes, I *did* plan it. Strategically. But the feeling behind it?"

She shook her head, a small, disbelieving smile tugging at her mouth.

"That surprised me."

She leaned back slightly, eyes lifting to the ceiling for a beat before settling back on the camera.

"I've spent a long time being angry at Jonah," she said quietly. "And when you're angry for that long, it becomes... useful. It gives you structure. Something to hold onto."

Her fingers tightened together.

"But anger is exhausting," she continued. "And when he told me the truth—when I realized that what happened was both of us getting swallowed by something bigger—I couldn't keep holding it the same way."

She swallowed.

"The kiss?" Brittany said, voice softer now. "That wasn't about winning the show. Not really."

She met the camera's gaze directly.

"It was about choosing not to be frozen anymore."

A beat.

"And yeah," she added, a breath of humour slipping back in, "I won't pretend I didn't know exactly what it would do to the room."

Her smile faded again, replaced by something raw and vulnerable.

"But what scared me?" she admitted. "Is that when Jonah kissed me back, it didn't feel like acting. It felt like coming home to a place I thought I'd lost the right to want."

She laughed quietly, shaking her head.

"That should terrify me," she said. "And it kind of does."

She paused, then added softly, "But it also feels... honest."

The storm groaned against the walls, distant but relentless.

Brittany squared her shoulders.

"For the first time in a long time," she said, "I'm not doing this out of spite or fear."

She smiled—small, real, steady.

"I'm doing it because I want to see what happens next."

By the time the storm eased off, it was late afternoon.

Not the bright, triumphant kind of clearing you saw in commercials, but the quieter version. The wind dropped first, backing off in reluctant stages. The howling faded into a low murmur, then into nothing at all. Snow still drifted lazily past the windows, thick flakes floating down like the world had decided to exhale.

Inside the church, the chaos rearranged itself into something gentler.

People drifted into clusters without discussion, instinctively. Kids sprawled on the floor with coloring books and half-built towers. A few locals sat near the stove, mugs cradled in their hands, talking softly about weather patterns and roads that might or might not reopen by morning. Someone dozed in a chair, boots still on, head tipped back against the wall.

The film crew hovered at the edges now, subdued. The story had already happened. Anything else would be aftermath.

The New Couple

Jonah leaned against one of the support beams near the side wall, arms folded loosely, watching the room settle. His body still felt like it was humming faintly, adrenaline finally bleeding off after hours of intensity. Everything felt quieter inside him too. Not resolved. But steadier.

What surprised him most wasn't the calm.

It was Janessa and Trevor.

They sat in the far corner on a low bench, angled slightly toward each other, knees not quite touching but close enough to matter. No big gestures. No performance. Just conversation. Quiet, intent, real.

Janessa's hands moved as she spoke, slower than usual, less precise. She wasn't pitching. She wasn't explaining herself. She was just... talking. Trevor listened with his whole body, elbows braced on his knees, head tilted toward her, attention unbroken.

At one point she laughed—soft, surprised—and Trevor smiled back like it was something he planned to remember later.

Jonah blinked.

Huh.

He felt it before he saw her.

Warmth at his back. Familiar. Easy.

Brittany stepped in close behind him and slid under his arm like it was the most natural thing in the world. Like her body had always known exactly where it belonged, even when her head had argued otherwise.

Jonah inhaled sharply, then caught himself and let the breath out slow.

He dropped his arm around her shoulders without thinking, hand settling at her upper arm, thumb brushing lightly against the sleeve of her sweater. She leaned in just enough to make it clear it wasn't accidental.

Not that he was complaining. Not even a little.

She fit there like she'd never left.

That wasn't the surprise.

The surprise was that she was letting herself do it.

That she wasn't bracing. Or calculating. Or half-stepping away the second it might mean something. She stood there with him, weight relaxed, head tipping slightly toward his chest, like she'd decided this moment was allowed.

Jonah stared out at the room, afraid to move too much, afraid to break whatever fragile truce she'd made with herself.

"Looks like the storm broke," he said quietly, more observation than conversation.

"Outside," Brittany replied, voice low and warm against his ribs.

She followed his gaze to the corner. Watched Janessa and Trevor for a beat.

"Well," she murmured, lips twitching, "that's unexpected."

Jonah huffed a soft laugh. "Right?"

Brittany tilted her head, thoughtful now. "She's not pretending."

"No," he agreed. "She really isn't."

They stood like that for a moment longer, sharing the view. Sharing the quiet.

Around them, life resumed in small, human ways. Someone laughed. Someone dropped a mug. A kid announced they were hungry again despite having eaten less than an hour ago.

Normalcy crept back in, careful but persistent.

Brittany shifted slightly, her hand sliding around Jonah's waist, fingers resting there with casual certainty. He felt it like a promise he wasn't going to name yet.

"Hey," she said softly.

He glanced down at her. "Hey."

She didn't look up right away. Just stayed there, tucked in close, eyes on the room like she was grounding herself in it.

"Thank you," she said finally.

"For what?"

"For staying," she replied. Then, after a beat, added, "For not pushing. For letting things be what they are right now."

Jonah's chest tightened.

"Anywhere else would feel wrong," he said simply.

She looked up at him then, really looked, something warm and unguarded in her eyes.

"Good," she said.

And she stayed right where she was.

They lingered at the back of the group as everyone funnelled toward the doors, the room dissolving into a tangle of coats, boots, chatter, and shouted reminders about gloves.

Janessa stood with her parka draped over one arm, staring at it like it had personally betrayed her.

Trevor noticed.

He didn't say anything.

No quip. No commentary. No sideways grin about symbolism or storms or emotional arcs.

He just stepped closer.

"Here," he said quietly.

Janessa looked up, startled—not by the offer, but by the tone. Soft. Unassuming. Like he wasn't trying to make a moment out of it.

He took the coat from her hands and held it open, patient, waiting.

She hesitated for half a second.

Then slipped her arms into the sleeves.

Trevor lifted the collar gently, careful not to tug her hair, fingers brushing the back of her neck by accident. He stilled immediately, like he was checking in without words.

She didn't pull away.

He settled the coat properly on her shoulders, tugged it down just enough to sit right, then reached for the zipper.

"Okay?" he asked.

Janessa nodded, throat tight in a way she didn't quite understand.

He zipped it slowly, deliberately, stopping just below her chin so she could adjust it herself if she wanted. No crowding. No claim. Just consideration.

For a moment, neither of them moved.

The noise of the room faded around them, swallowed by the simple intimacy of the act. Janessa's hands curled briefly around the front of the coat, grounding herself.

"You're very good at this," she said quietly.

Trevor blinked. "Trevor is good at coats?"

"At noticing," she replied.

Something crossed his face then. Surprise. And something gentler beneath it.

"I try not to assume," he said simply. For once not talking about himself in the third person.

She let out a breath she hadn't realized she'd been holding.

"Thank you," Janessa said. Not for the coat. For the space.

Trevor nodded once, like he understood exactly what she meant.

When they turned toward the door, they walked side by side, close but not touching.

And for the first time in a long while, Janessa didn't feel like she was being watched.

Back to Normal(ish)

They made it back to the production house after an hour-long drive that felt like 3 hours.

The storm hadn't fully released them yet, but it had softened—less fury now, more persistence. Snow still fell, thick and steady, blurring the edges of the road, but the wind no longer screamed its objections. It felt like the world had decided to tolerate them again.

By the time they pulled in, everyone was quiet in that way people get after surviving something together. Tired, but not depleted. The house lights glowed warm against the white, windows fogged from heat and life and the promise of food.

Hot showers happened in staggered waves.

Steam curled down the hallways. Trevor used up all the hot water and apologized loudly. Steph claimed she "liked a bracing rinse anyway," which no one believed. When Brittany finally pulled on soft clothes and padded back into the main room, her hair still damp, she felt the tension in her shoulders ease for the first time all day.

Jonah was already there, sleeves rolled, hair still slightly wet, leaning against the counter and talking quietly with Janessa about something utterly unimportant. He glanced up when she entered, eyes softening immediately, like his body had clocked her before his brain caught up.

She smiled before she could stop herself.

Dinner was ready by the time they all regrouped—simple, hearty, comforting. The kind of meal that didn't try to impress. It just wanted to feed people.

There were only four of them now.

The reality of that settled gently over the table as they sat down. The next elimination was in the morning. If the weather held. Even Steph had limits, and sending someone home in a full blizzard apparently crossed them.

Dinner was quieter than usual.

Not awkward. Not tense.

Just... settled.

Without discussion, they naturally paired off.

Trevor and Janessa sat close, knees angled toward each other, voices low. And Brittany found herself beside Jonah, their legs brushing beneath the table, his presence a steady, grounding thing.

For a few minutes, there was only the clink of cutlery and the low murmur of conversation.

Then Trevor looked up, eyes flicking between Brittany and Jonah with the mild curiosity of someone who'd noticed something and wasn't sure whether to poke it.

"You know," he said casually, "Trevor sensed real feelings when you and Jonah got married last night."

Brittany groaned instantly, dropping her head into her hands.

"Oh my God, Trevor."

Janessa bit her lip, clearly fighting a smile.

Steph's head snapped up. "You got married?"

Brittany made a sound that might've been a protest or might've been a prayer.

Jonah didn't miss a beat.

"Well," he said calmly, spearing a potato like this was a perfectly normal conversation to be having, "it was a very serious ceremony. Conducted by a married woman with a dish towel. There were vows about storms and dogs. A spoon was involved."

Paige blinked. "A spoon."

"For symbolism," Jonah clarified.

Steph burst out laughing. "I leave you alone for one blizzard—"

"There were witnesses," Jonah continued, unruffled. "Several children. Dolls. A tiara."

Trevor lost it, laughter spilling out of him.

Paige shook her head, laughing despite herself. "I can't believe I missed that."

"It was very exclusive," Jonah said dryly. "You had to be emotionally trapped by weather."

The table dissolved into laughter, the kind that loosened something tight in the chest. Brittany looked up, relief washing through her as the attention shifted fully away from her.

She felt Jonah's leg press more firmly against hers beneath the table.

On impulse, she squeezed his leg, fingers tightening briefly through the fabric of his pants. A silent thank you. A quiet *you saved me.*

He glanced at her, eyebrow lifting just slightly.

She smiled.

And she didn't even care when the cameras zoomed in on the movement.

Let them see.

Steph letting them sleep in was wrong.

Not wrong in a *kind* way. Not wrong in a *production finally developed empathy* way. Wrong in a way that made the back of Brittany's neck prickle. Like the air before a storm. Like when your phone alarm didn't go off and your first instinct wasn't relief but suspicion.

Jonah noticed it too. She could tell by the way he checked his watch twice, then looked toward the hallway as if expecting Steph to burst in yelling about lost footage or "missed magic."

Instead, nothing.

They gathered for breakfast slowly, the house unusually quiet. No PA shouting times. No producer voices murmuring in corners. Just clinking cutlery and the low hum of the heater fighting the cold. Brittany sat across from Jonah, steam rising from her mug, and for a moment it almost felt... normal.

Which was the most alarming part.

Steph arrived precisely three minutes after everyone sat down.

She didn't walk in so much as *bounce.*

She practically vibrated with excitement, clutching her clipboard to her chest like it was the Holy Grail. Her eyes were bright. Too bright. The kind of bright that suggested either caffeine poisoning or a terrible, beautiful idea.

"Children," she announced, beaming. "We just got permission to participate in the annual dog sled race."

The room froze.

Brittany felt it immediately. That drop in her stomach. That familiar tightening in her chest. Jonah's gaze snapped to hers at the exact same moment, their eyes locking in a silent, shared *oh no*.

Steph plowed on, oblivious or simply uninterested in their fear.

"Toklo reached out," she continued, pacing now, clipboard hugged tight. "Said the community loved you all—of course they do—and wanted to have you join them. Authentic! Local! Snow! Dogs!" She made a little helpless sound of joy. "It's tomorrow. Starts early. Toklo will set you up with the sleds and the dogs, and I will get you all fitted with GoPros."

Jonah's brows knit. "GoPros."

"Yes," Steph said reverently. "First-person POV suffering."

She clapped her hands once, sharp and delighted. "We're heading back up to the village in twenty minutes so you can learn all about mushing. You'll be staying there overnight, so pack smart."

She paused, glowing.

"This," she said softly, hugging the clipboard tighter, "is going to be better than *Eight Below*."

The silence that followed was immediate and absolute.

Brittany felt Jonah's foot brush against hers under the table. Not accidental. Grounding. A quiet check-in.

Because *Eight Below* hadn't had a happy ending.

The dogs froze to death.

The humans cried.

Everyone learned a lesson they didn't ask for.

Steph, meanwhile, sighed dreamily. "I can already see the montage."

Brittany swallowed, eyes still locked with Jonah's.

A dog sled race.

In the Arctic.

On camera.

Together.

She wasn't sure if she wanted to laugh or run.

Jonah's mouth curved just slightly, the barest hint of a smile. The kind that said *we'll survive this* even if he wasn't entirely convinced.

"Well," he said quietly, "at least we won't be standing still."

Brittany exhaled. That was the problem.

Battle-Ready

Getting ready took exactly twelve minutes and felt like preparing for a military extraction.

Steph was suddenly everywhere.

She paced the entryway with her clipboard tucked under one arm, walkie crackling at her hip, hair pulled back so tightly it meant business. Any lingering softness from breakfast was gone. This was Producer Steph. Battle-ready. Eyes sharp. Voice loud.

"Okay, listen up," she barked, clapping once. "Janessa, Trevor, you're in car one. Brittany and Jonah, other car. Paige, I want batteries triple-checked. Mics stay hot. No one leaves anything behind. Let's do this, people. It is going to be..."

She stopped mid-sentence.

They all did.

Steph's eyes went glassy.

Just for a second. A shimmer. A breath caught too high.

"...gorgeous," she finished softly.

The word hung there, reverent and sincere.

Then she ruined it immediately.

"Paige," she snapped, fingers flicking. "Move faster. This isn't a spa retreat."

Paige scrambled. Another PA bolted. The moment shattered, but Brittany saw Jonah's mouth twitch, like he'd caught it too. That brief, unguarded awe Steph never wanted anyone to see.

The drive took about an hour. Snow stretched endlessly in every direction, the landscape stark and stunning in a way that made Brittany's chest ache. Jonah kept his gaze out the window most of the way, quiet but alert, like he was memorizing the place.

When they pulled into Toklo's village, he was already waiting, bundled up and grinning like he'd won a bet.

"You guys were better than HBO," Toklo said cheerfully as he helped them haul gear from the vehicles. "I've had three aunties ask if you're coming back next season."

Steph beamed like she might combust.

The camera crew moved fast. Mics clipped. GoPros mounted. Batteries checked again because Steph watched them do it with unsettling intensity.

Then Toklo waved them forward.

"Come on," he said. "Time to meet the dogs."

They followed him toward the kennels, the air sharper here, filled with sound. Barking. Howling. A restless, electric energy that vibrated under Brittany's skin.

Toklo stopped and turned to face them, expression shifting from friendly to serious.

"Okay," he said calmly. "These are not pets."

Janessa's face fell.

"Well," Toklo added, "not during the winter. So don't expect them to lick your faces or beg for treats. They will try to bully you."

Trevor blinked. "The dogs?"

"Yes," Toklo said pleasantly. "Don't let them."

Brittany felt Jonah's shoulder brush hers. Solid. Steady. The dogs barked louder, straining against their lines, eyes bright and eager.

This wasn't a show anymore.

This was something real.

The dogs hit them all at once.

Sound first. A wall of it. Barking and howling and that sharp, high-strung yipping that vibrated straight through Brittany's ribs. The ground seemed to hum under their boots as the dogs strained forward, muscles bunching, lines rattling, breath steaming in wild, impatient clouds.

Janessa took one step back.

Trevor leaned in, eyes wide. "They look like they could sense weakness."

"They can," Toklo said. "They will."

Steph made a small, delighted noise and gestured frantically for cameras to keep rolling.

Toklo clapped once.

Sharp. Precise.

The sound cut through the noise like a blade. The dogs didn't fall silent, not really, but the chaos tightened, pulled inward. Proof that they could listen if they felt like it.

"Good," Toklo said mildly, as if they'd passed a test no one else had seen.

He moved briskly between the two sleds, checking lines, tugging harnesses, nudging dogs back into position with practiced ease. Tails wagged. Teeth flashed. One dog leaned hard into the line, vibrating with anticipation.

"Passengers first," Toklo said without looking up. "Men in the sled. You'll switch halfway. Women drive."

Brittany stilled.

Jonah swung into the sled easily, relaxed but alert, like this kind of thing fit into him without friction. Trevor followed suit on the second sled. Janessa climbed in beside him, already laughing, nerves leaking out sideways.

Toklo straightened and finally faced them.

"Rule number one," he said. "The dogs want to run. Always." A pause. "You are not here to motivate them. You are here to guide them."

Brittany nodded, filing the words away carefully.

Toklo stepped up behind her and placed the handlebar into her hands.

She froze.

"They're going to pull," Toklo said calmly. "Hard. If you lean back, they win. If you panic, they win. If you shout"—his mouth twitched—"they laugh at you."

Janessa squeaked. Loudly.

Brittany tightened her grip.

"Stand tall," Toklo continued. "Soft knees. Let them feel your weight without fighting it."

Jonah leaned forward slightly. "You've got this," he said, quiet and certain.

Toklo clocked the exchange immediately. "Good. You two listen to each other. That matters."

He crouched to fix a twisted line. One of the dogs snapped playfully at his mitten.

Toklo didn't look up. "You," he told the dog, mildly, "are not in charge."

The dog sneezed in his face.

Toklo stood. "See? Negotiation."

They started slow.

Which was what Toklo called it.

To Brittany, it felt like controlled chaos. The sled lurched forward, sudden and alive. She yelped, boots skidding before she found her balance.

"Don't fight it!" Toklo called. "Let them pull you into motion!"

"I AM IN MOTION!" Trevor yelled from the other sled as Janessa shrieked.

"Brake!" Toklo barked. "Brake means stand on it, not think about it!"

Janessa screamed again. Their sled fishtailed. Steph let out a sound that might have been joy or terror or both.

Brittany's heart slammed against her ribs. Cold air burned her lungs. The dogs surged, powerful and eager and absolutely unstoppable.

And something clicked.

She leaned forward.

Not against them.

With them.

The sled steadied. The lines smoothed. The dogs responded instantly, rhythm settling in like a shared breath.

Jonah laughed, breathless and surprised. "There you go."

Brittany smiled, wide and unguarded. "I like them."

They practiced turns. Stops. Starts. Toklo's voice cut clean through the noise.

"Talk less."

"Commit to the line."

"Trust the dog who knows the trail."

"And don't look scared. They can smell that."

By the end, Brittany's arms ached. Her face burned with cold and exhilaration. Jonah looked alive in a way she hadn't seen in a long time. Not since before everything had gotten careful. They switched and the men got their turn at driving. The men found out it was not as easy as it looked and all four of them learned to respect the dogs, the sled and the skills needed to guide the dogs.

Toklo approached as they unhooked the dogs, his expression thoughtful.

"You two don't rush each other," he said indicating Brittany and Jonah. "That's good mushing."

Brittany blinked. "It is?"

"Yes," Toklo said simply. "Fast teams break. Good teams finish."

Jonah exhaled slowly, like the words had landed somewhere deep.

Toklo smiled then, softer. Warmer.

"Tomorrow," he said, "remember this. The dogs already know how to run." A beat. "You just decide how."

Race Morning

Race morning arrived without ceremony.

No dramatic wake-up call. No music cue. Just the low blue light creeping through the windows and the muffled sound of dogs already awake, already ready. Brittany lay still for a moment, listening to the house breathe around her. Someone shifted down the hall. A floorboard creaked. Somewhere outside, a dog barked once, sharp and eager.

She felt awake in a way she hadn't for years.

Not nervous. Focused.

They layered up in silence, breath fogging the air as they stepped outside. The village was already moving. Headlamps bobbed. Fires burned low and steady. Sleds lined up like promises, runners glinting faintly under fresh snow.

Toklo met them near their team, hands tucked into his coat, expression calm as ever.

"You sleep?" he asked.

Jonah nodded. "Enough."

Toklo accepted that. He handed Brittany her gloves, checking the fit with a practiced tug.

"Dogs are good," he said. "They know today is different."

Brittany glanced at the team. They strained against their lines, muscles coiled, eyes bright with anticipation. Not anxious. Certain.

Steph hovered just outside the frame, whispering furiously into a headset.

"GoPros live in thirty," she hissed. "I want breath. I want frost. I want that look people get when they realize they can't quit."

Brittany ignored her.

Jonah got into the sled, just like they had practiced.

Toklo's gaze flicked between them.

"Remember," he said quietly, so only they could hear. "You don't race the other teams. You race the trail."

Brittany nodded. Jonah did too.

The call went out. Sleds moved into position. The noise swelled, dogs screaming their joy into the cold.

Brittany took the handlebar.

The weight was immediate. Alive. Expectant.

"Ready?" Jonah asked.

She inhaled. The air burned. Cleared her head.

"Yes."

The signal came.

And suddenly they were flying.

Snow blurred beneath them. The dogs surged forward, powerful and precise, the sled skimming effortlessly behind them. Brittany leaned into the motion, reading the trail the way Toklo had taught her, adjusting without thinking.

Left.

Now.

Easy.

Jonah moved with her, shifting his weight in perfect counterpoint to keep the sled balanced. They didn't speak. They didn't need to.

They weren't leading.

They weren't lagging.

They were... right.

Brittany laughed once, breathless and surprised by it. Jonah heard her and smiled, wide and unguarded.

Ahead, the trail opened. Snow stretched endless and clean, tracks weaving forward into possibility.

For the first time in a long time, Brittany wasn't chasing anything.

She was exactly where she needed to be.

Toklo had warned them about this stretch.

Not dramatically. Just a quiet note, delivered the way he delivered everything important. *The lake looks solid here. Mostly. But don't rush it.*

The trail curved slightly, the wind sharper now, the ice beneath the runners singing in a low, hollow way that made Brittany's stomach tighten.

"Okay," Jonah said. "Let's switch."

They slowed together, instinctive and smooth. Brittany slid into the passenger spot on the sled, heart still pounding from the pace, while Jonah took the handlebar. He planted his boots, tested the brake, and shifted his weight.

"You good?" he asked.

She nodded, pulling the blanket tighter around her legs. "Yeah. You're up."

They started again, slower now. More deliberate. Jonah's posture changed immediately—focused, alert, reading the surface instead of the clock.

That's when it happened.

A sharp crack split the air ahead of them.

Not loud. Not explosive.

Just... wrong.

Another sled—twenty yards ahead and slightly to the right—lurched sideways. The ice beneath it darkened, spiderwebbing outward in a jagged line. One of the dogs yelped as the front runners slipped, the sled tipping, runners skidding toward a widening seam of black water.

"Stop!" Jonah shouted.

He didn't wait to see if anyone listened.

He slammed the brake and leaned back hard, the dogs responding instantly, skidding to a halt just short of the fracture. Brittany was already out of the sled, boots digging in, pulse roaring in her ears.

Trevor and Janessa had been close behind and they stopped too, their sled fishtailing before Trevor wrestled it still.

The ice groaned.

The other team's sled broke through first—one runner disappearing, then another. Water surged up, dark and fast. The dogs thrashed, terrified but tangled, lines pulling them dangerously close to the edge.

Brittany dropped to her knees, spreading her weight flat against the ice, crawling forward inch by inch. Jonah was beside her immediately, mirroring her movements without a word. Trevor followed, then Janessa, eyes wide but steady.

"Human chain," Jonah said calmly. "Spread out."

They linked arms, bodies low, breath coming fast and white in the cold. The ice creaked beneath them, protesting but holding.

Brittany reached first.

She grabbed the nearest dog's harness, fingers numb, heart hammering as the ice dipped again. Jonah braced behind her, boots dug in, Trevor anchoring him, Janessa gripping Trevor's coat with everything she had.

"Easy," Brittany whispered, more to herself than the dog. "I've got you."

Together, they pulled.

Slow. Careful. No jerking. No rushing.

One dog slid free, then another, claws scrabbling as they were hauled back onto solid ice. Trevor scooped them up, dragging them clear, voice low and steady now, all commentary gone.

The musher came next, soaked to the knees, shaking violently as Janessa grabbed his jacket and hauled him back inch by inch.

The ice cracked again.

Brittany froze.

"Hold," Jonah murmured. "Just hold."

She did.

They did.

And then they were all back—soaked, breathless, dogs whimpering but alive—sprawled in a shaking heap on safe ground.

For a long moment, no one spoke.

Then Trevor let out a shaky laugh. "Okay," he said hoarsely. "That was... objectively bad."

Janessa nodded, eyes bright. "We're never speaking of this again."

Jonah looked at Brittany, hands still locked around her wrists, grounding, present.

"You okay?" he asked.

She nodded, throat tight. "Yeah."

And she meant it.

They were wet. Shaking. Breathing hard.

And they still had over an hour left to go.

The adrenaline burned off fast, leaving cold in its wake. Brittany's gloves were soaked through, fingers already stiffening. Matthew and John were worse—teeth chattering violently, lips pale, clothes heavy with ice water. Hypothermia wasn't a looming threat. It was already knocking.

The dogs, at least, were holding.

They'd shaken most of the water from their thick coats, steam rising off them as they stamped and whined, confused but alive. Strong. Ready to move if asked.

"We don't wait," Jonah said. "We move. Now."

There was no argument.

The decision came together in seconds, the way good ones did.

Brittany stepped forward first. "I'll drive their sled."

Janessa nodded immediately. "I'll ride with you. Less weight for the dogs to pull."

Matthew and John barely protested as Jonah and Trevor pulled them toward the other sleds, wrapping spare layers around them, activating hand warmers and shoving them into their numb hands.

"You're passengers," Jonah said firmly, already rearranging weight, checking lines. "No heroics."

Trevor shot him a look. "Never thought I'd hear you say that."

"Shut up and drive," Jonah replied with a smile, but his voice was steady, focused.

The roles locked in.

Brittany took the handlebar of the damaged team's sled, feet planted wide, forcing warmth back into her legs through motion. Janessa in the passenger spot, eyes on the dogs, hands ready to adjust harnesses if anyone faltered. The men split up in the other two sleds.

They'd move together.

No passing. No splitting up. No pushing ahead.

As fast as they safely could.

They started again, runners biting into the snow, dogs surging forward with renewed purpose. Brittany leaned into the rhythm, guiding rather than forcing, reading every shift in the ice, every change in wind.

The cold was brutal now.

It clawed at her lungs, numbed her face, threatened to steal focus if she let it. She didn't. She couldn't.

This wasn't about winning anymore.

It wasn't about time.

It was about keeping everyone upright. Breathing. Alive.

Ahead of them, the trail stretched long and unforgiving.

Behind them, the ice groaned and settled, as if disappointed they'd escaped it.

They kept moving anyway.

Together.

Purpose

The change didn't come all at once.

It crept in quietly, settling into Jonah's bones sometime after the medics stepped back and the adrenaline finally loosened its grip. When his hands stopped shaking. When Matthew met his eyes, lucid and grateful. When John squeezed his arm once, hard, like he needed Jonah to understand something without words.

Jonah had never felt so present.

Not on a podium. Not under lights. Not being admired or desired or expected to perform. This had been different. Necessary. His body doing exactly what it needed to do, his mind clear, his choices mattering in real time.

He replayed it over and over in his head.

The weight of Matthew against him. Counting breaths. The certainty that if he stopped paying attention for even a second, something would slip.

He had been useful.

Not impressive.

Not charming.

Useful.

The realization landed with a quiet force that surprised him.

For the first time in his life, he felt proud of himself — not for what he had, or where he came from, but for what he'd done.

Across the truck, Brittany stared out the window, the village lights fading behind them.

She felt different too.

For years, she'd held onto the idea of becoming a social worker like a lifeline. It had always made sense. Helping people. Making a difference. It was a clean, noble path, one she could explain easily to herself and others.

But what she'd felt out there on the ice hadn't been theoretical.

It had been immediate. Physical. Urgent.

She hadn't helped because it was her plan.

She'd helped because someone needed her — and she hadn't hesitated.

The clarity of that startled her.

Maybe social work was still the path. Maybe it wasn't. What she knew now was simpler and harder to ignore.

She wanted to be where things *mattered*.

Where presence counted.

Where people didn't fall through the cracks because no one was watching.

The celebration afterward was overwhelming.

The village gathered around them like they'd done something sacred. Food appeared from nowhere. People hugged them without asking. Elders clasped their hands and spoke softly, eyes shining. The dogs were fussed over like heroes, which they were.

It was too much. Too warm. Too bright.

The drive back was quiet.

Not uncomfortable. Not strained. Just full.

Jonah leaned his head back against the seat, eyes closed. Brittany rested her forehead against the glass, breath fogging the window.

Neither of them spoke.

They didn't need to.

Something had shifted.

And whatever came next — it wouldn't look like what they'd planned.

But it would be real.

Jonah broke the silence first.

"I think I want to do something like this," he said quietly. "For real."

Brittany turned toward him. The truck's interior light caught her eyes, still bright, still a little stunned by everything they'd just lived through.

"I was just thinking the same thing," she said. Then she let out a soft, incredulous laugh. "But what, though? Firefighters? EMTs? Search and rescue? I don't even know where you start with something like that."

Jonah smiled, the kind that came when he wasn't trying to be anything other than honest. "Me neither."

The truck hit a small bump in the road, jostling them closer together.

"But," he added, glancing at her, voice suddenly careful, "did you want to figure it out together?"

The word *together* hung between them.

Brittany felt the reflex rise fast and sharp. The old instinct. *I don't need this. I don't need saving. I don't need to tie my future to someone else's.*

Her mouth opened.

Then she stopped.

She thought of the ice.

The chain of hands.

The way no one had been the hero — just present.

She slid her hand into Jonah's, not gripping, just resting there.

"No matter what happens with this show," she said, steady now, "I want to try."

Jonah's fingers tightened gently around hers.

Not in promise.

In agreement.

Outside the window, the road stretched on, dark and uncertain.

For the first time, Brittany didn't feel the need to know exactly where it led.

She just knew she was willing to walk it.

Epilogue

In the end, Janessa and Trevor won.

They had the votes for the biggest changes, and honestly, they deserved it. Somewhere along the way, Trevor had stopped narrating his life in the third person—mostly—and Janessa had shown up as herself. Not louder. Not sharper. Just real. The version of her that stayed.

They took the win with equal parts disbelief and joy.

Jonah and Brittany went back to Toronto.

Not triumphantly. Not with a plan carved in stone. Just... committed. They enrolled together at the local community college for EMT training, figuring it was a good place to start. A way to learn how to show up when things went wrong. A way to be useful.

They didn't know if they'd stay EMTs forever.

They didn't need to.

When the show aired, they hosted a viewing party from Jonah's parents' living room. His family crowded the screen in squares and rectangles, laughing and wincing and asking too many questions. Trevor and Janessa joined from halfway across the world, sunburned and dusty and unmistakably happy.

Still together.

Still building schools in Africa.

Trevor announced—proudly, sheepishly—that he'd landed the occasional voice-over gig for a local TV station doing nature documentaries. Brittany laughed until she cried, because of course he had.

They watched themselves on screen like strangers they knew very well.

People who'd been colder. Younger. Less certain.

When the credits rolled, no one rushed to log off.

There were jokes. Promises. Plans that might happen and some that wouldn't.

Later, after the house went quiet, Brittany leaned into Jonah on the couch, their legs tangled, the future still unwritten but no longer frightening.

They hadn't won the show.

But they'd found something better than a prize.

A direction.

And the willingness to keep choosing it.

Steph got her BAFTA.

She cried.

She pretended she hadn't always known.

And she never made another first season that sucked.

A Heartfelt Thank You

I wanted to take a moment to say thank you to everyone who has picked up one of my books, left a review, recommended it to a friend, or even just quietly added it to their reading pile.

Writing can be a very solitary thing. Publishing is not. It takes readers—curious, kind, open-hearted people who are willing to spend their time and energy with a story that may or may not be what they expected. I'm incredibly grateful that some of you chose to spend that time with mine.

Thank you for being here. Thank you for reading. And thank you for making this all feel real.

Warmly,

Tasha Zima

About the Tasha Zima

Tasha Zima grew up trading romance novels with her mom like sacred artifacts, rereading dog-eared paperbacks until the spines gave out. She never expected to write one herself—until a small-town girl with too much pride and not enough sleep marched into her head and refused to leave. That girl became Katie, and However Much or Little, her first novel, poured out like a love song she didn't know she'd been humming for years.

Tasha has been married since 1997 to her first real love—a man with enough patience to weather her moods, and enough insight to see her clearly, entirely, and always. His steady presence is the best part of her life (even if he can't fold a fitted sheet to save his soul).

They live in a small town in New Brunswick with a dog, a cat, and an ever-expanding list of inside jokes. All three of her housemates are male, so she's dramatically outnumbered and fighting the patriarchy one sarcastic eyebrow at a time.

Follow Tasha on her website: www.tashazima.com and on Instagram @zima.writes

Ashby Lake Novels

All Ashby Lake books can be read as standalones, though returning characters and shared history may add extra depth if you read more than one.

Erin and Adrian

Nothing Too Fancy (Book One)
Nothing Too Tame (Book Two)
Nothing Too Perfect (WIP) (Book Three)

Katie & Bennett

However Much or Little (Book One)
Looking Up (Book Two)
No Matter What Happens (Book Three)
Everything All at Once (WIP) (Book Four)

Amy & Julian

FWB: Friends with Baking (Book One)

Vivian & Noah

Between Breath and Breaking (Book One)

Between Time and Terror (WIP – Title TBD) (Book Two)

The Tropes Series

Lakeweed, Lust & Longing

Lies, Cleavage & Quantum Theory

Confessions, Hot Tubs & Second Chances

Standalones

The Making of a Storm

Frogs, Fireworks and Forever (Standalone, Ashby Lake)

View all books and formats:

books2read.com/TashaZima

Join the Ashby Lake Reader List for bonus scenes and first looks from Ashby Lake:

https://books2read.com/author/tasha-zima/subscribe/1/2247031/

www.ingramcontent.com/pod-product-compliance
Lightning Source LLC
LaVergne TN
LVHW090935080826
845145LV00003B/753

* 9 7 8 1 0 6 9 9 8 1 0 4 2 *